Provided

by

Measure B

which was approved

by the voters in

November, 1998

THE
VERDICT ON WINTER

THE
VERDICT ON
WINTER

Eileen Dewhurst

SEVERN
SH
HOUSE

This first world edition published in Great Britain 1996 by
SEVERN HOUSE PUBLISHERS LTD of
9–15 High Street, Sutton, Surrey SM1 1DF.
First published in the USA 1996 by
SEVERN HOUSE PUBLISHERS INC., of
595 Madison Avenue, New York, NY 10022.

British Library Cataloguing in Publication Data

Dewhurst, Eileen
  Verdict on Winter
  I. Title
  823.914 [F]

ISBN 0-7278-4888-7

Typeset by Palimpsest Book Production Limited,
Polmont, Stirlingshire, Scotland.
Printed and bound in Great Britain by
Hartnolls Ltd, Bodmin, Cornwall.

For Norma Watt, Norwich Castle Museum, gratefully.

Chapter One

The baglady seemed unaware of the group of young people smoking and sniggering in a relaxed circle at the back of the fire-gutted garage. She squatted near the opening where the door had been, huddled up with her head on her chest and her arms around her worldly goods, just far enough inside to be out of the icy wind.

But the fact that she was there at all was offence enough for one of the girls, who sauntered across to her, still giggling, and asked her what the hell she thought she was doing.

The baglady mumbled, looking up with glazed glaring eyes, and the girl aimed a kick through trailing skirts before turning away to rejoin her companions.

"Come on, Marlene! Why d'you do that?" one of the boys asked, but it was a lazy protest and the girl responded with a kiss, taking the cigarette from his fingers as she slumped down beside him on the sacking, drawing on it, and returning it to his smiling mouth.

As the boy inhaled, the baglady wavered to her feet. The girl made a threatening gesture, but the baglady turned her back on it and left the shelter of the garage doorway, clutching her bag to her chest with both hands as she moved away, still crouched low and walking with a shambling limp that was surprisingly speedy.

She was halfway across the waste land when the children saw her. They stopped their football game and swarmed towards her with whoops of joy, gathering small

1

stones and throwing them at her as they ran. One of the stones struck her on the temple and the gush of blood, brilliantly red in its grubby surround, brought the children to a standstill when they were almost upon her. The baglady staggered, shifted her bag to one side, put a hand up to her temple then held it out to the children. Blood dripped from between the fingers, and the children, terrified by their achievement, turned as one and scampered away from her as fast as their legs would go.

The baglady yelled after them, an inarticulate bellow of pain and rage, then rummaged in her bag for a scrap of cloth, which she held to her head as she set off again, walking lopsidedly now, with the bag half under an uncomfortably arched arm.

She was lucky to be so near the hospital, but her progress slowed as she approached it and she took a zigzag course up to the entrance to Casualty. Her injury must be concealed till she had been to the women's room – this was more important than being ejected as an undesirable – and in a hidden angle of the building she substituted the blood-soaked cloth for another piece before taking advantage of a surge of people through Casualty doors.

She saw the sign and hurried to where it pointed, her movements suddenly co-ordinated. A male voice shouted behind her but she ignored it and hurled herself gratefully behind the door and on into the large cubicle for the disabled, where, as well as sanctuary, there was the bonus of floor space, a private washbowl, and a mirror.

The tall, slim figure of Phyllida Moon – actress and temporary acting assistant to Peter Piper, owner of the Peter Piper Detective Agency – emerged from the cloakroom carrying a suitcase. She and Peter had both been delighted by the discovery that the baglady bag (empty) went into the folding suitcase as easily as the folding suitcase (folded) went into the bag. They appreciated that this enabled Phyllida to emerge looking entirely respectable from the bolthole into which the baglady had scurried.

Phyllida smiled ruefully at the embarrassed orderly shifting from foot to foot outside the women's room door, indicating the wad of paper towelling held to her head. She thought he was about to question her, but when he caught a glimpse of what she was concealing he expressed dismay and urged her towards Reception. When the woman behind the counter saw her wound she told Phyllida she would be attended to straight away.

A young doctor and a nurse joined her in the cubicle after a mere quarter of an hour.

"What on earth have *you* been doing to yourself?" the doctor asked her as he examined her wound, looking interested to hear her answer.

"The corner of a cupboard," Phyllida explained. "I didn't fall, I just walked into it. I was lucky, I wasn't on my own, so I got a lift to the hospital."

"And away from it?"

"A taxi."

"I should, if I were you." A searching look. "Now, I'm not calling your nursing ability into question, but I'm going to clean it out."

The process was painful, and the nurse gave Phyllida her hands to hold. She managed to keep her protest to a murmur.

"Okay, that's it." The doctor grinned at her. Phyllida had to admit to herself that it was an admiring grin. "You're lucky, there's no flesh to stitch, so you shouldn't have a scar. Don't touch the dressing and keep it dry for five days, then come back to see us. Can you remember when you last had an anti-tetanus injection?"

Phyllida couldn't, so he gave her one, repeating the words "the corner of a cupboard" and looking at her

3

quizzically as she managed not to flinch – from the needle or his straight gaze.

"That's right," she said as he anointed the puncture. "The corner of a cupboard. I'll make that appointment."

"I should take some paracetamol or aspirin, too. You're likely to get a headache."

By the time she was sitting in front of Peter's desk the headache was raging.

Peter was shocked by her appearance. "Above and beyond the call of duty, as Jenny might say." He smiled at Jenny Timmis, his young, pretty and astonishingly competent receptionist, typist and bookkeeper, in case she might think he was taking the mickey, but she was too upset by the look of Miss Moon. Peter had invited her and his equally young, full-time assistant in the field Steve Riley into his office, feeling that Phyllida's bandaged, white-faced arrival at the Agency merited a general explanation of her condition. In any case, he was too soft to resist their pleading eyes.

"It was just bad luck. Some children threw stones as the baglady crossed the waste land, and one hit me where it bleeds so easily. I'd just had such good luck – if you can call bad news good luck – I shouldn't complain."

"You aren't doing," Steve said.

"Bad news." Peter repeated. "So the Robinsons were right to be suspicious. Their son *is* part of the group?"

"I'm afraid so. He's even being smiled on by the dreaded Marlene. And I watched him smoke. I'll let you have my report tomorrow."

"Which may just deter him from going on to the hard stuff. Thank you, Phyllida, and well done. A medicinal scotch has never been more appropriate." Peter smiled at Jenny and Steve as they got to their feet, pleased that as usual they had cracked his code. He disliked confrontation, preferring to run his business if possible with politeness and harmony. "So. Case closed," he said,

4

with the closing of the door, sighing and trying to look sombre. When the outcome of a case was unhappy he always found himself with a slight struggle on his hands between satisfaction at a job well done and regret for the contents of the report he must deliver. "D'you want a rest?"

"Over the weekend?"

They exchanged grins. "You're sure that's all you need?"

"Yes. And I'll have the bandage off by Monday."

"You're a heroine. Something's just come in that could be interesting. . . . How much time d'you have left?"

"Filming starts the middle of April. That means a couple of months, if I give myself a week or so to see about a flat near London. Only renting – I'm now the proud owner of the house I've been renting here. The sale's just gone through and 8 Upland Road's mine, Peter."

The expressive face lit up. Thin and permanently sun-burned under the flop of corn-coloured hair, 30-year-old Peter's face was still the face of a boy. "That's wonderful! I hope it means you'll come back to me between your TV assignments. And of course if. . . ."

"When the assignments come to an end," Phyllida helped him out. "Unless I go back to the stage, I'd love to." She was aware of a deep-seated anxiety being laid to rest.

"If you become one of these actresses who's always turning up on TV," Peter said, "you may not want the stage again. But you've got a second career here."

"Thanks. And thanks for the title."

"That's what it is, isn't it?"

"Yes." She hadn't thought about it until that moment, she had seen herself as she imagined Peter saw her, as she had first been: an actress trying to enhance a role by some hands-on experience. But in telling her it was more

5

than that for him he had told her it was more than that for her. The part of a private eye in a TV series had seemed the best thing life could offer her, but this was as good. The compensation for frozen emotions was proving rich.

"Yes, it is."

"I don't think you should tell your TV cronies about it," he advised.

"I don't think I can, if I want to keep it going."

This second career, in its unique way, was as vulnerable as the first. "I'm just realizing that the only way I can be sure of keeping my anonymity is to keep what I do here secret. My – friends – in the Independent Theatre Company know I'm working for a detective agency but not that I sleuth in character, and anyway I don't have much contact with them these days." Phyllida had been going to say *my husband*, but after just four months staying on alone in Seaminster her marriage to the company's stage manager seemed so long dead the word *friends* had come out instead. "The only person who really knows what I do is my ex-producer Ken Hatfield, who got me the TV break, and he's on my side."

Peter looked gleefully conspiratorial. "I think you should keep it that way. Life's absolutely full of coincidences and if you were the victim of one it would, well . . ."

". . . Kill my second career. It hangs on my being anonymous, doesn't it?" Phyllida Moon was on the Agency's books, but no one in Seaminster outside it knew she worked there apart from John Bright, manager of the Golden Lion Hotel across the square. Peter had identified a gang who were systematically robbing John's clients, and since the arrival of Phyllida on Peter's staff, the Agency had a back room in the hotel at her exclusive disposal, for those times when it was easier or more appropriate for her to change or sleep at the hotel than to go home, and when she needed an address to give a suspect or a place to escape from one. Since Phyllida had joined the Agency a string of women had checked in and out of the Golden Lion and answered the telephone to a number of clients, a nightcap or a breakfast tray beside their bed. "If I once lose my most effective disguise of all, I'm done for."

"Your undisguised self?"

"That's it." And done for in two senses, perhaps. There had already been times, like that very afternoon, when reversion to Phyllida Moon had been her escape from the danger into which one of her characters had shambled. "You said there was something interesting?"

"Possibly. I had a maturely attractive widow in this morning, to tell me her worries about the brother she shares a house with."

"Yes?" As always, as she settled into Peter's small armchair to hear about her next assignment, Phyllida was aware of a shot of adrenalin. If they hadn't already done so, the shots could become addictive. And were already helping her postpone unwelcome but increasingly insistent thoughts about what that undisguised self of hers amounted to. . . .

"Brother and sister both appear to be in a comfortable way, and live together but separately in a large house in Marlborough Drive. I gathered they get on well and it suits them – he's divorced and her two children are grown up and away. She does upmarket good works and he's number two in the Snaith Gallery in Moss Street. I expect you've discovered it, it's Seaminster's most prestigious. A bequeathment to the town from one of it's wealthy, art-mod citizens. Old Masters, Victorians, Pre-Raphaelites, Impressionists, and a very few moderns."

"I've sighed over a few things in the windows," she said.

"I thought you might have. Well, everything seemed fine, Mrs Dinah Everett told me, until the other morning

7

at breakfast, when her brother opened a letter that very obviously upset him. He put it in his pocket without showing it to her or saying anything about it, and when she asked him what it was he mumbled that it was just some tiresome thing to do with work. But she'd collected the post from the hall carpet and noticed the envelope and the address – cheap manilla and illiterate-looking capitals. The fact that he was trying to hide its effect on him worried her, and when it all happened again a few days later, and this time he crumpled the letter up and dropped it beside his plate, she'd worried herself into an instinctive cunning that rather impressed me. Very resourceful, I thought. She said 'I'll just tidy up,' or something like that, and swept letter and envelope and the debris of her own post into a plastic bag already full of rubbish destined for the bin, and went outside with it before he'd properly realized what she was doing, extracting the letter on the way. When she came back he looked uneasy but didn't say anything, and she had an idea he might be thinking of looking in the bin later. So she went out to it again with tea leaves and potato peelings and so on to try to make the remaining papers irretrievable. She told me with a smile that it went against her conservationist principles and confirmed my instinct that she's a well-balanced lady and what she said was probably a fair rendering of what had happened."

"How had the brother been between letters?"

"Good question. The first letter changed him" – Peter glanced down at the notes in front of him – "turned him nervy and irritable. That was what seemed to worry her more than the letters themselves."

"Did she show you the second one?"

For answer Peter pulled a stout manilla envelope from under his sheet of notes, extracted a thin, crumpled envelope from it with a pair of tweezers and, separately, a thin fold of creased white paper, which he

8

opened out with the tweezers. He swivelled to face Phyllida.

She read the thick dark capitals aloud. ' "FAKE WINTER? SEEMED LIKE A GOOD IDEA, DIDN'T IT? BUT YOU WON'T GET AWAY WITH IT." ' She looked up, puzzled. "I don't understand it, but it doesn't sound as unlettered as it looks."

"No. And it sounds even less so when you know what it means. Mrs Everett explained that her brother's the Snaith Gallery's expert on the Pre-Raphaelite Brotherhood. There's a painter called Frederick Sandys who was on its fringes and whose work was very much influenced by its methods. I hadn't heard of him." Peter raised a questioning eyebrow, a one-sided accomplishment which Phyllida, smiling at herself in her bathroom mirror, had tried unsuccessfully to emulate.

She shook her head. "Rossetti, Millais, Holman Hunt. That's as far as I go."

"That's as far as anyone goes, strictly speaking, Mrs Everett told me. But every movement has its peripheral characters, and after he had made friends with Rossetti, Sandys apparently became a very faithful one. He announced his intention of painting the four seasons and completed *Autumn*, which is in the Castle Museum's collection at Norwich, along with a pen and ink sketch for *Spring*, which it was thought he had never got round to working up. Then, six months or so ago, *Spring* arrived anonymously at the Snaith Gallery in full oil-painted Pre-Raphaelite splendour. Just there, among the parcel post one morning, franked at Seaminster's head post office – where no one, of course, has any memory of who brought it in. Her brother – David Lester – was beside himself with excitement. He thought the picture was right, but of course it had to go through all the usual tests. It passed them, and was introduced to the public as the Snaith Gallery's very own final version of *Spring*,

9

as advertised by the artist himself. A couple of months later, *Summer* arrived, and was also authenticated. The gallery sold the pair for something around fifty thousand, and David Lester earned fat commissions. *Winter* arrived recently and is currently undergoing the tests. Lester received the first anonymous letter a day or two after it had gone to the experts, and the second a couple of weeks later. *Winter*'s under wraps, by the way – like the others were until they were pronounced genuine. All the gallery staff were asked to make a promise of secrecy to the director, and Mrs Everett's certain her brother didn't tell anyone about it apart from herself. She's also certain he isn't guilty of the scam if there is one – she insists she's not biased in his favour, she just knows him too well – but at the same time she's uneasy that the accusation in the letters should have had such an effect on him and can't understand why he doesn't just go to the police and ask them to investigate a nuisance. The first two pictures have been authenticated and, anyway, it's not as if Lester discovered them himself, or tried to pass them off as genuine without submitting them for all the proper tests."

"Perhaps he *did* discover them. He could have posted them to the gallery as well as anyone else."

"We didn't discuss that possibility, but I'm sure it was in her mind as well as in mine. And making her feel uncomfortably disloyal."

"Why, though, if the pictures are the real thing? All he'd be guilty of would be eccentricity."

"Or pathological modesty. Yes. But the threat in the letters is for what comes next."

"So what does his sister want from you?"

Peter shifted in his chair, beginning to look uncomfortable himself.

"She has to go away for a week," he said, turning towards the window as he spoke. There was certainly a lot to look at, Phyllida thought exultantly, her own glance crossing the complex of low roofs beyond the buildings the far side of the square and alighting on the pale winter sea, touched yellow by a clouded sun. She hadn't got used to the bounty of her own newly-acquired home in a real place after an adult lifetime of theatrical digs and short-lived tenancies, and hoped she never would.

When she turned back to face Peter his eyes left the seascape and looked reluctantly into hers. "Although she can't believe her brother guilty of the accusation in the letters, she's realist enough to recognize that if he is he could take advantage of her absence to do some illegal business at home. And it could be that the letter-writer might come into the open, particularly with the brother on his own."

"So she wants him watched."

"Yes. I told her I could do better than that." Peter turned back to the view. "I asked her if she had a cleaning lady and she told me she had a contract with one of those outfits that send strong young women in twos and threes to scour their way through a house once a week. I suggested she tells them to hold their horses while she's away and takes on a daily, which would be more suitable for her brother on his own and could be presented to him as a coup – she's managed to get hold of a friend's treasure during the friend's absence. They live such independent lives they don't know all about each other's friends, so that should work. Then I said I could call on someone who would fill the bill." Peter's expression now contained an element of pleading. "Light morning cleaning – as I said, Mrs Everett's only away for a week and if I've read her aright the place will be spotless – and leaving an evening meal ready to heat up. Keeping eyes and ears open and reporting to the Agency anything and everything seen and heard beyond the crunching of the breakfast toast."

"Someone you could call on?"

"Yes. Will you? Just for a week?"

"Yes."

"Phyllida, you're pure gold." She matched his relieved grin. "I thought it was better not to present you as a member of my staff, better she saw you as an informant than a professional sleuth. Agreed?"

"Oh, yes."

"Good!" Peter hesitated. "I told her I'd try to offer more coverage than that, as well."

"More coverage than that?"

"It *is* going to be rather time-consuming if it takes off as it could," he said apologetically. "Before I left, Mrs Everett remarked jokily that it was a pity I hadn't another person I could call on who would be capable of working as a receptionist at the Gallery, seeing that they were wanting a temporary replacement for a girl who was taking leave to have a baby. I didn't respond to that, I just said I'd see if I could offer more coverage." Peter and Phyllida stared at one another. "If you feel you could manage both," he said at last, leaving the sentence unfinished. "We'll be covering both parts of David Lester's life," he resumed triumphantly, as Phyllida nodded. "It'll have to be afternoons only, but I know how persuasive you can be." They exchanged smiles again, both remembering how Phyllida had persuaded Peter to take her on after his initial rejection of her: by presenting herself the second time as an elegant, mysterious, Lauren Bacall-like client whom he had failed to recognize until she reverted to her own unobtrusive, introverted self.

"When do I start in the house?"

"If you could go and see Mrs Everett on Monday? If you feel well enough, of course," Peter added hastily. "She's going away late Monday afternoon."

"Just as well the Robinson case is wound up."

He was relieved to see that she was still smiling. "I

12

know. Thanks. So far as the gallery's concerned – choose your own moment."

"I might do that on Monday, too."

"You really are splendid. I mean it. Names, addresses, telephone numbers." He pushed the usual thin file across the desk to her. "I expect we'll all still be here on Monday round about six if you feel like looking in. . . ."

Chapter Two

This time the baglady was alone in the garage, and more uneasy than when she had shared it with the smokers. She was crouched at the back where they had been sprawling, and there were reefer stubs round her skirts. The square of daylight was still framed in burnt twisted metal, but it was slowly disappearing behind a descending grey door. The baglady wanted to get out but she couldn't move, she could only watch the door steadily come down. And she couldn't call for help, her throat was as paralysed as her legs. It was only when the door reached the ground and the horror was more than she could bear that she managed to make a supreme effort and run screaming down the long dark tunnel of pain into which the door was transformed.

Phyllida heard the scream, felt the seeping relief of realization that she was at home, in bed, and the pain a dead arm coming to life via pins and needles. But the nightmare had been so vivid it was moments before she could move, be certain she was out of the tunnel and delivered from evil.

She had intended spending Saturday the way she usually spent it when Agency business allowed – cleaning, gardening, writing a few more paragraphs of her ongoing history of women and the theatre, perhaps driving somewhere and then walking – but, as she found herself able to move in spite of her afflicted arm, Phyllida decided to respect the shivering lassitude she had dismissed the night before and accept that her first experience as a baglady had been clinically traumatic. The nightmare was still too close for her to consider going straight back to sleep, so she went down to the kitchen and brought tea and toast up to bed, reading a few pages of newspaper before drifting dreamlessly into unconsciousness.

By midday she was enjoying herself, and when in the late afternoon she was sated with sleep, she raised her pillows and lay watching the curve of the bay until all she could see was the thin white edge of the tide and the reflected taper of lights coming on in the buildings at the foot of Great Hill.

When Great Hill had disappeared into the starless sky she put on a dressing-gown and went downstairs and watched television, an activity associated with enforced occupation of the small room at the Golden Lion rather than the sitting-room of 8 Upland Road. But now she was relishing the peculiar pleasure of convalesence: idleness without guilt.

On Sunday, though, she was willingly at work again. By midday she had completed her report on the Robinson case, and after a sandwich and coffee she went walking beside a sullen grey sea in search of a woman Mrs Everett would be happy to present to her brother as a borrowed treasure who could be relied on to clean the house and prepare his supper satisfactorily during her week's absence.

Phyllida had decided early in her stage career that the farther both a character and an appearance were from her own the easier they were to play, and she soon discarded the idea of a modern-style career cleaner with a good education behind her. By the time she was home again she had settled on Mrs Emily Cookson, a widow who, at fifty-five, was probably too young to have worn curlers in public, although her mother might well have done so, in the southern equivalent of Coronation Street

15

where Emily had been born and brought up. Emily's hair was a heavily permed greying wig which transformed Phyllida, rehearsing into her cheval glass, even before she had applied the rosy, shiny make-up, tied the strings of her flower-sprigged overall, primmed her lips and made her mental transition. An archetype verging on caricature, Mrs Cookson was going to be one of her easier characters. And whatever the ease or difficulty of any of her off-stage roles, they were always less fraught when she was playing to people who had never met Phyllida Moon.

The staff of the Snaith Gallery hadn't met Phyllida Moon either, and Anita Sunbury, the Lauren Bacall look-alike to whom she owed her job with Peter, had already been created. But Mrs Sunbury possessed a number of qualities both physical and mental, the lack of which in her own persona Phyllida lamented. She knew that consistent presentation of this confident sophisticate would be a tightrope compared with the wide pathway along which Mrs Cookson would make her unswerving way. When she had assumed the wig, clothes, make-up, facial expression and inner certainty of Mrs Sunbury's ripe self-assurance, Phyllida's relief at how well they still worked was mixed with regret that she was unable to do for herself what she could do for another woman. She spent the remains of the day thinking out the strategy of Mrs Sunbury's reactions, and left the tactics of Emily Cookson to her instincts.

In the morning, she discarded her bandage and reassumed Mrs Cookson's brisk, no-nonsense persona. It was a miserable day, cold, wet and windy, and she took a rare taxi, leaving it at the end of Marlborough Drive and scurrying past three large, detached, between-the-wars houses before turning in at the Everett/Lester gate. The Cedars, at least in its front garden, boasted only one tree to justify its name, but it was as fine as any domestic specimen Phyllida had encountered and dominated the arc of lawn. The house was older than the houses she had passed, Edwardian Tudor in bright black and white above red brick, the date 1903 carved into the canopy of the porch she was glad to reach.

Being of the old school, Mrs Cookson, despite the weather, had first tried the side gate, ringing the front doorbell only on finding herself unable to get round the back. The type of woman Phyllida had instinctively expected was quickly there, advancing to the step in a profusion of long slender limbs.

"Ah! Mrs Cookson. What a morning! But you're admirably prompt. Please come in. Perhaps you'd like to hang your coat in here." Mrs Everett opened a door just inside the house and indicated a vacant hook. She had a measured smile, as if she had made a decision to exercise it, but it was still attractive, as was her low, soft voice. And Phyllida had to admire the detailed perfection of her appearance, navy blue jacket over navy blue skirt and quietly multi-coloured silk blouse; the cloud of carefully careless ash-blonde hair.

"I tried to go round the back," Mrs Cookson said. She spoke with the local sub-London accent. "But the gate was locked."

"Most women these days wouldn't even have tried it." Mrs Everett looked impressed, and Phyllida told Mrs Cookson to disregard the assumptions in the word *women*.

"The younger ones perhaps," she responded. "But I'm not young. As you can see."

"You look fit enough. Please come through." Mrs Everett led the way across the large, expensively furnished hall, her walk complementing its proportions. In what had to be the smallest of the entertaining rooms, she sank into an armchair with the nestling aplomb of the woman Phyllida looked forward to resurrecting that

17

afternoon in the gallery. "Do sit down, Mrs Cookson."
Mrs Cookson took the edge of an upright Regency-style
chair. Phyllida suspected it of being the real thing. "Now,
I understand you are prepared to do more than a daily
help usually does."

"I work for Dr Piper," Mrs Cookson said, as if
repeating the words a hypnotist had told her she would
say when she came to. "I do what he or his client asks me.
And clean and polish properly," she added defiantly.

"I'm taking *that* for granted. I just want to tell you –
what else I need. Dr Piper thought it best to leave that
to me. To save time and be sure we get it right."

It was time to be co-operative. "Very sensible, I'm
sure. So you just tell me, now."

Mrs Everett was suddenly bewildered, realizing herself on strange and delicate ground. "You know the
background, Mrs Cookson?" she asked hopefully.

"I can say I do." Mrs Cookson didn't actually put a
finger against her rosy nose, but her expression implied
possession of a seat at the conspirators' table. "Dr Piper
filled me in on that. Just as far as was necessary," she
added reassuringly. "He showed me the letter."

Mrs Everett's frown disappeared. "Good. It's painful
for me to be spying on my brother" – the shudder
passed noticeably down the length of her body – "but
whoever is writing and sending these anonymous letters is sick and I'm worried for David's safety." Mrs
Everett hadn't justified her request in this form to
Peter, and Phyllida suspected she had thought it up,
perhaps come to believe it, since contacting him. And
the writers of anonymous letters were always potentially
dangerous.

"Of course you are." Mrs Cookson's smile was measured too, but lacked the charm of Mrs Everett's. "Now,
I gather you've looked in drawers? Cupboards? Any
known or suspected hiding places?"

"Exactly." Mrs Everett's relief eased her embarrassment. "That – side of things – has been taken care of. What I would like from you" – Mrs Everett's distaste for her self-imposed brief was all at once keeping Mrs Cookson at arms' length with a pair of invisible tongs – "is – well, your eyes and ears! Just – being here!" The hauteur collapsed in a real and helpless smile, and Mrs Everett relaxed. "Unfortunately, our post arrives early, before my brother goes to work. But he's hardly likely to be on his guard with you as he is with me, and you should have a chance to see what he does with any – further letter. We have to hope he won't put it in his pocket. If there's a second post it always arrives before noon. Dr Piper told me you know how to – to open and then reseal an envelope." Mrs Everett couldn't bring herself to meet Mrs Cookson's eye.

"I do."

"Good. I'm sorry it's all mays and mights. The telephone may ring. My brother may come home during the morning. Someone may call. Another letter may arrive. On the other hand, nothing may happen at all."

"That's what Dr Piper told me," Mrs Cookson responded, unfazed.

"Good," Mrs Everett repeated. Her legs were crossed and she began to circulate a long slender foot, looking down to watch its movement. "You'll understand, Mrs Cookson," she said hesitantly. "It isn't that I don't trust my brother. It's just that . . . with his safety being at stake I have to take every precaution."

"Of course you do. It's very wise of you. Don't worry, Mrs Everett, I can see how it is."

Phyllida was aware of the effort as Mrs Everett at last looked her in the eyes. "I believe you can," she said, getting to her feet. "So we have no need to prolong this interview. It's just a week, you understand. I expect you could do with your wages now."

"I could, and that's a fact." Mrs Cookson's grin was Phyllida's as well, in relief at this evidence that Mrs Everett, having met Mrs Cookson, continued to believe she was dealing with a charlady with a sideline rather than a professional sleuth.

"Here you are, then. As agreed with Dr Piper. He told me you'd prefer cash." Mrs Everett counted out notes, closely watched by Mrs Cookson, who stowed them away in a zipped pocket in the lining of her large handbag.

"Thanks," she said as she snapped the bag shut. "Have a good holiday and don't worry."

"No unilateral action," Mrs Everett said over her shoulder as she led the way to the front door. "I mean," she said, opening it as Mrs Cookson reclaimed her coat, "don't try to do anything on your own. Report any and everything that happens to Dr Piper."

Mrs Cookson bridled slightly, and looked dignified. "That's what I've been told to do. So I'll do it."

The helpless smile reappeared and Mrs Everett shrugged, a graceful gesture. "Forgive me, Mrs Cookson, I know you will. This is new territory for me and I'm not at home in it."

"Of course you're not." Mrs Cookson's mollifying words were reinforced by Phyllida's own sudden sympathy. "But don't worry, now."

"I'll try not to."

It was quite a walk to the gate, but when Phyllida turned after opening it Mrs Everett was only just shutting the front door.

"Can I help you?"

Words and smile were automatic, but the girl behind the Louis Quinze desk was too unaffectedly pretty for them to be off-putting, and the young man who had entered the Snaith Gallery at the same time as Anita

20

Sunbury gulped and stuttered as he said he just wanted to look round.

"Sure." The girl's dark-rimmed eyes had been on him to the exclusion of Mrs Sunbury, and shifted slowly as he moved reluctantly away. Phyllida saw them take her in, and the girl come slightly to attention as a look of admiration flitted across her flawless face. So far so good. "What can I do for you?" the girl asked, a shade less impersonally.

"I've just come to look round too, I'm afraid." An intensification of the mild interest as the girl heard the husky American voice. "It all looks so good from the windows, and it's better still inside."

The girl shrugged. "It's okay, I suppose."

The tall, slim woman with the air of chic and the attractively ravaged face smiled as she looked round the space she was gracing. "Shouldn't you be showing a bit more enthusiasm, young lady?"

The girl's smile this time was different – spontaneous and slightly embarrassed. "Yeah. And I might get to like it. Art, I mean."

"So how come you're here if you don't like it yet?"

"I'm a temp, my agency sent me. It was a toss-up between this and the bowling alley on Heaton Street. I thought this would be less rough." Now the smile was a grin. "It's that all right. But maybe I'll find myself with more to do when Sonia goes off."

"Sonia?" Phyllida saw Anita Sunbury as an all-round magnet of a woman, attracting female confidence as well as male attention. It looked as if she could be right.

"The senior receptionist. She's having a baby any minute and everyone's in a tizzy. Of the stiff upper lip variety, or course." The girl had covered her local burr with an exaggeratedly posh accent, and she and Mrs Sunbury both laughed. They looked round the serene space in which a client and a salesman murmured

21

together in front of a tiny, dark landscape in a large gold frame, and two women whispering their opinions of a Belle Epoque promenade in Impressionist parkland. The young man had wandered out of sight, into one of the smaller galleries invisible from the road.

"So you'll be in charge when she goes?"

The girl grimaced, putting on a shudder. "You're joking. They're getting another temp. Or two, if they can't find one with experience. You all right?"

Mrs Sunbury had put her hand to her breast and taken a sharp breath. Hardly crowd-pulling gestures, but Phyllida could see that she now had the girl's full attention.

"I'm fine. Perhaps never better. Look – I'm the widow of an Englishman with time on her hands, and I'd just love to be reminded what it's like to work in an art gallery."

"That'd be great!" For the first time the girl was really animated, even let Phyllida see the double take. "Hey! You say reminded?"

"Believe it or not" – and this girl would, at least – "I used to own one. Light years ago, back home in the States."

"You did? It's just what – You've got to see Mr Carrington! The gallery owner! I'll ask him—" The girl's hand was already out towards the telephone complex.

"Hang on a minute. Let me get my breath." The girl now was staring at her anxiously. "Look, I wouldn't want to put your job on the line unless you really wanted to leave."

"You wouldn't be, I told you, they want extra help. Two people if necessary, but if it was you they'd only want one. And I don't suppose I'd want to leave, if you were here."

"You're very flattering, honey. What's your name?"

"Deborah. Deborah Handley."

Mrs Sunbury drew a deep breath and threw back her

22

beautifully casual fair head. "Very well, Miss Handley, please tell the master I'm here. Just say there's a Mrs Sunbury you think he might be interested to meet," she went on, as Deborah flicked a switch. "To do with temporary help during – is it Sonia's? – absence."

Deborah said almost that, then looked up at Phyllida as she replaced the receiver, her eyes sparkling. "He's coming out! He's lovely, by the way." The girl's face was respectful and admiring, totally without lust. "Everybody loves him."

"That's nice," Mrs Sunbury commented. As she stood waiting, Phyllida was wearing her character like an overcoat to conceal the sagging of a nervous body. This was a crucial moment, and she was very nervous.

Deborah was looking expectantly towards one of the two openings on to the smaller galleries, and in a very few moments a man came purposefully through it, a tall man in a grey suit with abundant grey hair and a grave smile. The sort of man, Phyllida knew at once, whom even the bolshiest employee would find it hard to cheek, yet who carried an aura of approachability and potential understanding.

He nodded to Phyllida, then turned to the girl behind the desk. "This is Mrs Sunbury, Deborah?"

Deborah made a nestling movement in her chair, Phyllida suspected because the most senior member of the staff had remembered the name of the most junior. "Yes, Mr Carrington. She's American and she used—"

"I think it would be more helpful if Mrs Sunbury spoke to me herself, Deborah." There was no reproach or put-down in words or tone, and Deborah's "Sorry" left her excitement intact.

"I understand Miss Handley has informed you of our need of a temporary replacement in Reception? That's all right, Deborah," he continued swiftly, aware from Deborah's face and her catch of breath of her sudden precipitous descent from cloud nine. "I welcome initiative. Perhaps you'd like to come through to my office, Mrs Sunbury?" Mr Carrington's gentle manner and grave smile were unvarying, and gave Phyllida no clue to his reaction to her performance.

"Thank you." Mrs Sunbury nodded gratefully to Deborah and strolled by the Director's side into the gallery from which he had appeared. He came to a halt between two sombre-centred gold frames and opened a door identifiable by no more than parallel hairline cracks between upper and lower dado and a small gold knob above a gilded lock.

Behind the door was the elegantly restrained comfort of a low modern suite in pale gold, flanking a low glass table and matching pale gold walls, and an old-fashioned french window on to a very small stone-flagged courtyard set with urns and two white iron seats. As Phyllida saw it the flags were beginning to darken with the rain that had just managed to hold off over lunchtime.

"So," Mr Carrington began, motioning Mrs Sunbury to one of the low chairs and standing looking down at her, his back to the only classical component of the room, a tall marble chimney-piece carved in a high relief of goats' heads and swags. "Miss Handley told you there was a temporary vacancy in the gallery for a receptionist, and you said you were interested? Would you like to tell me more?"

She told him what she had told Deborah, with elaboration. Then, trying not to sound as breathless as she felt, she told him she was still convalescent from surgery and was under doctor's orders to spend most of the morning in bed.

"So I'm afraid it would have to be afternoons only, and I know you want someone for the whole day. I'd

24

love to work at the Snaith Gallery, but of course I understand—"

"I think the afternoons will suit us very well, Mrs Sunbury. I don't anticipate any difficulty in finding someone for the mornings. Both posts are temporary, as I think you already appreciate."

"I do. And thank you." It was hard to stop Anita's grateful smile from widening into Phyllida's relieved grin.

"Good." He mentioned a salary, which Phyllida accepted with amusement at her relief that it was too low to bring Anita into a tax bracket and necessitate the production of some official proof of her identity.

"Good," he said again. "When can you start?"

"Now?" she suggested, letting the grin have its way. "I mean, officially tomorrow, but perhaps I could spend the rest of this afternoon . . . ?"

"An excellent idea!" the Director said approvingly. He looked at his watch. "A quarter past three. I'll get my secretary to take you to the staff room, and if you spend half an hour over a cup of tea you should meet most if not all of the other members of the team. And Thelma will see to the arrangements for your payment." He touched a gold bell beside the fireplace.

It was answered quickly by a small, stout lady somewhere in her fifties. She had neat brown hair a little too richly coloured to be natural, no ring on her plump left hand, and a pleasant round face with brown eyes that fixed themselves immediately, and with what looked like anxious affection, on the director.

"This is Miss Royle, my secretary and my right hand," he told Mrs Sunbury, and Phyllida noted Miss Royle's discreet bridle of gratification. "And this, Thelma, is Mrs Sunbury, who's going to help us out in the afternoons during Sonia's absence. If you can take her now to the staff room she should meet most of the other members

25

of staff as they come in for tea. And then Sonia can show her the ropes."

"Of course, Mr Carrington. I'm very pleased. . . ." But the brown eyes were wary and appraising. "If you'd like to come with me, Mrs Sunbury."

"Sure, honey." Phyllida was amused to see appraisal give way to simple interest as Anita spoke, and by the time they had strolled and chatted the length of the other side gallery and entered a room dominated by easy chairs, Thelma Royle's reserve had disappeared.

"Meet Sonia Waring, our senior receptionist," she said, pointing to an attractive girl lying back in an armchair, then crossed the room to test the heat and weight of a large teapot. "Sonia, Mrs Sunbury's the first half of your order of release. A pity you can't come in the mornings," she said to Anita. "Milk and sugar?"

"A very little milk, thanks, no sugar. And my name's Anita. I'm sorry about the mornings." Phyllida told the two women what she had told the director. "But I'm okay," she ended, "I won't faint on you, or anything like that."

"Sonia needs to get away *now*," Thelma Royle stressed severely, "if she isn't to have her baby in the gallery."

"If I can get the general hang of things this afternoon," Mrs Sunbury suggested, "she could at least start going home at lunchtime." The senior receptionist's stomach was so large it looked like an extraneous object someone had parked on her where she lay sprawled.

"Thanks!" In her pleased surprise Sonia Waring dragged herself upright. "I'm ready when you are."

"Mr Carrington suggested we start in here, so that Mrs Sunbury can meet – Ah, Pamela." Thelma broke off as another woman came into the room. "This is Anita Sunbury, who's going to fill in for Sonia in the afternoons. Anita, this is Miss Pamela Bennett, our expert on the Impressionists." Phyllida thought there was a slight emphasis on the word *Miss*, but she was already inclined to believe Miss Royle capable of generating the bile which could lead to the production of anonymous letters.

But not so obviously as Miss Bennett, an aggressively unadorned youngish woman with a pasty face and unruly straight hair escaping from the comb by which it had been inadequately anchored.

She nodded in response to Anita's greeting, stared at her for a few moments, then marched across the room to help herself to a mug of tea, which she carried out of the room on another nod.

"She's always like that," Sonia said lazily. "But she's all right." Miss Bennett had passed a man in the doorway without acknowledgement on either side. "David!" Sonia exclaimed, as he made for the tea. "I've got half a replacement! This is Anita Sunbury, who's going to fill in for me in the afternoons. Anita, this is David Lester."

"Hello," Anita drawled, as David Lester stared through her. Phyllida was struck by how well he fitted his sister's description of a man consumed by anxiety, and only then registered the slight figure, wavy brown hair and pale, classic-featured face. The hair was tidy, the suit fitted and the tie was straight, but David Lester radiated disarray.

"Oh. Hello."

"David's our expert on the Pre-Raphaelites," Thelma told Anita.

"Ah. I've always hoped—"

"Another time, if you'll excuse me," he said hurriedly. "There's a telephone call I have to . . . I hope you'll be happy here." Even that had been an effort, Phyllida noted as he hastened away, mug in hand.

Thelma and Sonia gazed after him thoughtfully. "He never seems to have his tea with us these days," Thelma

27

began, but Sonia interrupted as another, younger, man entered the room.

"Philip! Philip won't carry his tea away with him, will you, Philip?"

"Today he won't!" the man responded, staring with open admiration at Anita. His aura of relaxation was as obtrusive as David Lester's anxiety, and he was taller and darker, with strong features and sleepy brown eyes. Anita gazed steadily back at his challenge, and Phyllida was half grateful and half afraid at being able to look her fill at the first man for as long as she could remember who had stirred her senses.

Thelma broke the spell, introducing Philip Morgan, modern art specialist, and explaining Anita's presence.

Thoughtfully, his eyes still on her, he repeated her name.

"Hello, Philip," Anita said, then turned to Sonia. "Perhaps we should get started, honey, if you're going to take tomorrow afternoon off."

"It wasn't as unfraught as it sounds," Phyllida said later in Peter's office, looking away from Steve's fascinated gaze. If she had remembered before calling in at the office how Mrs Sunbury had bewitched him in her first incarnation she would have gone first to the Golden Lion and discarded her. "Mr Carrington seemed relaxed and ready to listen, the archetypal busy person who always has plenty of time, but his eyes were so watchful I never got rid of the feeling they could see past my lies."

"They didn't, though," Jenny stated anxiously.

"Evidently not. I spun my yarn about the gallery my husband and I had run twenty odd years ago in Wisconsin and, fortunately, it's a state he's never been to or had dealings with. Then I told him I'd sold up my home in Glasgow after being widowed and was staying at the Golden Lion until I decided where and in what

28

type of accommodation I wanted to live. I chose Glasgow because I've played there more than most places and got to know it a bit. Charles Carrington doesn't give anything away, but he took me on without asking for a reference, just made sure he got it over to me that the post is temporary. Deborah in Reception had told me they were prepared to take on two people if they couldn't find one sufficiently experienced, and they'll have to do that anyway with Mrs S only able to manage afternoons. Telling him that was when I really kept my fingers crossed, but he bought it. I think it helped that Mrs S had recently had surgery and the doctor had told her she wasn't strong enough yet to work a full day. And he'd have the comfortable feeling that with it being a temporary appointment Mrs Sunbury would be easy to get rid of if things didn't work out."

"Nobody would want to get rid of Anita Sunbury!" Steve's pale face had retained the flush which had spread over it with Mrs Sunbury's arrival, and he was eyeing her legs in a way he would never have eyed Miss Moon's.

Peter's eyes followed Steve's, then met Phyllida's in understanding. He got to his feet. "It's Miss Moon who requires a medicinal glass," he pronounced, looking at his watch. "And it's a quarter past six."

Steve and Jenny rose on an instant and moved to the door, Steve pausing before closing it to give Mrs Sunbury's nether regions a last lingering look.

Peter and Phyllida waited for the sound of the outer door before letting their laughter out.

"It's incredible, but it appears to be sex," he said when he was able.

"Poor Steve."

"Not so poor. His Melanie is loyal, however dull he finds her."

"It's only dreams," Phyllida said. "It's people without dreams I'm really sorry for." But she hadn't been sorry

29

for herself in the long years when she had had none. And now the TV series and her work with Peter had appeared, from way beyond her imagination. . . .

"Did you meet your subject?" Peter was asking. He had opened his drinks cupboard and begun to pour whiskies.

"Yes. And his sister wasn't exaggerating his state of mind. I also met an angry female expert on the Impressionists, and a relaxed young man who sees to the few moderns the gallery sells." Phyllida hoped her instant rapport with Philip Morgan wasn't visible in her eyes, and reminded herself it had been between him and Anita Sunbury. "There was also Mr Carrington's devoted secretary, and the very pregnant young woman I'm replacing. All I can say at this stage is that they strike me as being equally likely or unlikely to have written a couple of anonymous letters, but I've yet to meet Edward Brooke, who looks after Victorian genre painting. Cheers."

They raised their glasses, and over the rim of Peter's Phyllida saw the sudden chagrin in his expressive eyes.

"I'm so sorry," he said. "I haven't even asked you how you're feeling since. . . ." He leaned towards her, and with belated concern examined the small patch of dressing on her temple. "Are you all right? With the bandage gone and the plaster half hidden by the wig. . . ."

"I'm fine, I'd forgotten about it myself." She had. And wouldn't tell Peter, or anyone else, about the way she had spent the weekend.

"You're a trouper. I've been thinking about bringing Steve into this business, by the way. He hasn't got anything ongoing at the moment, and it might pay off to cover Lester's comings and goings. What do you think?"

"I think it's obviously a good idea."

"Next week, then. When you've finished at The

30

Cedars. If you haven't cracked it single-handed by the weekend, of course. Here's to tomorrow!"

"To tomorrow!"

As she raised her glass again Phyllida felt the adrenalin like the stab of a needle.

Chapter Three

"You'd better come in," David Lester said irritably. He wiped a crumb from the corner of his mouth with the table napkin in his hand. "Though why D bothered . . . I'm sorry, don't take any notice of me, I'm no good in the mornings." He flashed Phyllida a smile which transformed his anxious face, but the anxiety was back as he opened the cloakroom door and peered inside as if he didn't know what he might find. "You can hang your coat in there."

"Thanks." As she did so Phyllida glanced at the rosy face in its surround of frizzed grey hair, and was reassured to see it as a photograph rather than a mirror image. "I'm sorry I came to the front door," Mrs Cookson apologized for the second time, as she emerged tying her apron strings. "But the side gate's locked."

"I forgot you were coming, I'm afraid. And anyway . . . nobody thinks they should go round the back these days, do they? The gate's only opened for the binmen and the window cleaners." He was talking off the top of his head, but it had brought the smile back. A few strands of hair had fallen over his forehead, and his movements were jerky. "Kitchen this way. Sorry, you know, don't you. . . ."

When she had joined him beside the breakfast table he looked at her helplessly and spread his hands. "I'm afraid I'm not domesticated, and anyway I have to go. But my sister will have shown you the ropes." He looked hopefully at Mrs Cookson, who nodded. "Fine. So just. . . ." His gesture took in the small area of the centre table occupied by the remains of his breakfast toast and coffee, and he swept up a coffee cup and drained it. "So far as my supper's concerned there's some cold chicken, so if you could just peel a couple of potatoes and slice the beans. . . . It's all in the fridge. Don't fuss about the house, my sister killed all known germs before she left yesterday and I've made my bed." The smile again, but an obvious and continuous effort was required to concentrate on a matter outside the scope of his anxiety. "I'll see you in the morning, if you can manage to arrive the same time. If not, I'll leave you a note about supper. All right?"

"Fine." It was, it meant she could make the request which would enable Steve to help her if need overcame ethics. "Perhaps I should have a key, though? If you're happy—"

"Yes, of course. My sister left them ready." He had only to reach out. "Here you are. Now, is there anything else I've forgotten?" Her own rationed smile in place, Mrs Cookson shook her head. "Good. Don't be afraid to explore for what you need."

So it didn't look as if there was anything in the house for his sister to have missed. David Lester glanced at his watch. "Now I really must be off." The prospect appeared to increase his wretchedness.

"Yes. Of course. You work at the Snaith Gallery, don't you, Mr Lester? Your sister was telling me. I always like to look in the windows."

The smile this time was a rictus. "They're attractive, aren't they? Well, goodbye, Mrs er. . . . Those are front door keys, by the way. If you'll make sure the back door's locked from inside, then go out the front way and lock the mortice. . . . Thanks. I'll hope to see you tomorrow." In the doorway to the hall he turned back. "You can ignore the telephone," he said, his eyes huge with dread. "Or answer it and take a message if you feel strong enough." Not suspecting an audience, he had to be making the sick joke for his own entertainment. "It'll be for my sister, anyway," he said firmly, making a feeble attempt to square his shoulders.

He had told her that it might be for him. "Oh, I'll answer it. Off you go, now, I'll be right as rain."

Phyllida stood at the kitchen window until she heard the car engine decrescendo, looking down an orderly and extensive kitchen garden. She would have to be prepared for the arrival of a gardener.

When she turned away from the window she went straight for the two envelopes beside the toast rack, both torn roughly open. One was manilla, but there was a printed window address and when she put on the surgical gloves in her apron pocket and pulled out the envelope's contents she found a stockbroker's circular. The other envelope, small and white, contained a reminder that a dental appointment was due. Two letters addressed in handwriting to Mrs Everett were on the dresser.

Phyllida washed the few breakfast dishes, wiped plastic surfaces, dusted wooden ones, swept the floor. Beyond the kitchen it was easy to distinguish between the sister's domain and belongings and the brother's. Pride of the main sitting-room were a fine Queen Anne bureau and chest of drawers – Phyllida thought they were genuine – and a glance inside both made it clear that Mrs Everett had exclusive use of them. The small sitting-room seemed to be entirely hers, but there was another downstairs room of intermediate size, comparatively unadorned and with a masculine feel to it, the furniture heavier and the desk a large knee-hole. Two of the flanking drawers were locked, and Phyllida wondered if Mrs Everett had managed to get into them.

Upstairs the distinction was easier again. Mrs Everett had a pink and white bedroom en suite with a bathroom

34

full of elegant jars and bottles. David Lester's room was almost austere and his bathroom functional. The large guest room identified itself via a biscuit barrel and a bottle of spring water on the table between the two beds, a selection of books between bookends, and a wardrobe containing nothing but a satin evening dress and a set of tails, elegant but forlorn relics of a vanished way of life which left Phyllida, as she returned them to darkness, with a residual whiff of mothballs.

David Lester's assessment of the state of the house had been right, it was spotless. When Phyllida had wiped the ceramics in his bathroom and forced herself to dust horizontal surfaces and use the manual carpet sweeper here and there in his bedroom and on the landing, she went downstairs and made herself coffee.

Carrying it to the window, she saw a man in a flat cap bending down among the vegetables.

The weather was dramatically better than it had been the day before, dry and windless with a glow in the clouds indicating the position of the sun, and Mrs Cookson opened the back door and walked to where the kitchen garden began.

"Care for a coffee?" she called.

The man straightened up and stood silent, staring at her. He was tall and broad and in late middle-age. "Well, now," he said eventually. "You're something more like. You'll be the lady Madam's called in to look after her brother."

"You could say that," Mrs Cookson conceded. "Coffee, then?"

"Dash of milk, two sugars. Thanks."

"Don't let it go cold."

Phyllida went back into the kitchen and made the coffee in another mug. The gardener came in, removing his cap and wiping his boots elaborately on the mat inside the door, in time to take it from her hand.

35

"Just right," he said when he had sipped. "Strong enough. Can't do with weak coffee."

"Me neither."

"I'm Joe Daniels."

"Emily Cookson. Mrs."

"Pleased to meet you."

"Likewise."

"Not much for you to do 'ere, I shouldn't think," he said, smiling. His clothes were rough and dirty and his teeth needed attention, but something in his manner and his slowness of speech gave Phyllida the comfortable feeling that she was in the company of a real gardener rather than a handyman. "Madam keeps things right, and those young women. . . ." The gardener whistled, unlasciviously. "Madam told me she was laying them off while she's away, that you'll be keeping 'ouse and seeing to Mr Lester's evening meal."

"That's right. I'm leaving it for 'im. I 'ave to go at twelve. Another job."

His gaze was approving. "You work 'ard, you ladies of a certain age, if you'll forgive the expression. Not so many of you left. The young ones mostly don't 'ave the stamina, unless they prop each other up in a team. My daughter's always lying around. But my wife's like you. Works 'ard at 'er job, *and* when she comes 'ome. . . ."

It took Phyllida several minutes to break in and steer the conversation back to The Cedars.

"Mrs Everett's ever such a nice lady. Mr Lester seems nice, too, but sort of far away. . . ."

"That's it." The gardener stared down his domain, frowning. "It's new, you know. 'im being like that, 'e never used to be." He turned back to her, scratching the top of his head where there was a small natural tonsure. "I expect it's business, business isn't easy these days, is it? If it ever was. But when 'e's come down the garden these last few Saturdays to talk to me about what we're going

36

to do I've not felt 'e was really there, 'alf the time, if that makes sense." Mrs Cookson nodded sympathetically. "Off in some worry world of 'is own. I don't know. . . ." Mr Daniels shook his head, then brisked up. "Shouldn't be talking about me employer like this, I don't make an 'abit of it, but 'e's bothered me lately, and that's a fact. And *you* noticing it, too, and not even 'aving met him before."

"That's right," Phyllida lied. "Perhaps 'e's not well, or's 'ad bad news. 'as Mrs Everett changed, too?"

"I wouldn't say as she 'as, but she's worried about 'er brother. Even asked me the other day if 'e'd said anything to me. That's not like 'er at all, always civil, o' course, but just talking about the garden or asking me 'ow the family is. So she 'as to be bothered about 'im. I don't know," Mr Daniel said again.

"'as 'e said anything to you?"

"Not a word. Nothing much about the garden, neither. 'e usually 'as ideas, and I tell 'im mine, and we argue them out, but this past week or so 'e's just told me to get on with it as I think best. It's taken the edge off things 'ere, I don't mind telling you."

"I can see 'ow it would," Mrs Cookson agreed.

"Aye. Well. . . ." Mr Daniels rinsed his mug and placed it upside down on the draining-board. "I'd best be getting back to me vegetables."

"And I'd better take me duster round the sitting-room."

"Coals to Newcastle," Mr Daniels said mysteriously. He replaced his cap and opened the back door. "See you on Thursday, then. That's me other day. You coming every day?"

"Just for the week. Mrs Everett's back late Saturday. Ta-ta, then."

"Ta-ta. Thanks for the coffee. You got it just right."

The gardener closed the door behind him and Phyllida

went into the big sitting-room and began to repeat her lacklustre upstairs performance through the downstairs rooms. She kept the door to the hall open while she was preparing David Lester's supper, and when she heard the snap of the letterbox she ran out to see what had arrived – as eagerly, to her rueful amusement, as if she herself were expecting a love letter or a cheque. The second post was just one more white envelope for Mrs Everett, and when Phyllida changed her apron for her coat she had handled the telephone only to dust it and summon a taxi. As she settled into the back seat she had to remind herself that despite her sense of frustration she had already made the one vital discovery in this most intangible of cases: that Mrs Everett's concern for her brother did not stem from her imagination.

The Snaith Gallery was within short walking distance of Dawlish Square, across which the Peter Piper Detective Agency and the Golden Lion Hotel faced one another, and Phyllida had decided at the outset that the only remotely comfortable way for her to move between her dual roles was to spend the week in the hotel. Mrs Cookson having raised the eyebrows of three taxi drivers in the space of two days, she had also decided there would be less risk of being noteworthy for the rest of the week if she took her own car within striking distance of The Cedars. Once again she had dismissed her taxi at the end of Marlborough Drive, and on her second approach to the house had made a detour to investigate the narrow lane between two of the houses almost opposite, which she had noted as she had passed it the day before. It was wide enough for a small car, and when Mrs Cookson's stout brogues had negotiated the churned and rutted ground, Phyllida discovered that it widened into a space where a car could be parked out of sight of the road without blocking access. Whether it would incur the resentment of adjacent householders who might own the land was a danger she would have to risk. So far as thieves and vandals were concerned, Peter had assured her she would not be liable for repair or replacement for damage or loss incurred while she was on Agency business.

Upstairs in the small spartan bedroom at the Golden Lion, direct transformation from Mrs Cookson to Mrs Sunbury involved as dramatic a change of persona as Phyllida had yet made in one operation. But at least she was able to bypass her own reserve and go straight from one extrovert to another.

By the time she came out of the hotel, the sun had at last struggled clear of the cloudy sky and it was a conscious pleasure, as she walked from the Square to Moss Street, to have abandoned Mrs Cookson's purposeful bustle for Mrs Sunbury's leisured and graceful gait.

She found Sonia Harding at Reception. Sonia had a thin face, narrow shoulders and slim wrists, and until she struggled to her feet there was nothing to show why she was sitting at so far a remove from the Louis Quinze desk. She gave Mrs Sunbury a rueful but welcoming smile.

"Hello! Next time I get up from here it's going to be easier."

"Which means you've found someone for the mornings?"

"Yes. This really is my last day." Sonia's face was suddenly serious. "Until I'm ready to come back. I'm coming back."

"I know you are. And I'm leaving when you do, if not before. I don't want a career." Anita smiled, trying to lighten her reassurance.

Sonia responded as Phyllida had hoped. "Oh, I realise that, I wasn't warning you off. It's just that I suspected a gleam in the eye of my morning replacement. She told Mr Carrington she's wanted to get into the

Snaith Gallery ever since she went on her agency's books."

"And he told you. That was nice."

Sonia grinned. "Wasn't it? But I'm sorry you can't manage a whole day. Perhaps later?"

"Perhaps." But when her assignment at The Cedars was over Steve would be coming in. Peter would hardly want so much of both his assistants' time taken up with a single case, and Steve working part time in the street would offer more scope than herself full time in the gallery. Which reminded her that she must lend Steve the house keys while she was able. . . .

Sonia leaned her arms on the desk, her breathing audible. "Phew! I think I can't get any more uncomfortable and then I do. D'you feel ready to sit here? Deborah's on late lunch and you can hand over to her when she gets back if you like and go free-range. As I said yesterday, I think you'll make the better roving commissioner. Deborah does all right on the desk but she doesn't know anything about pictures or seem particularly keen to learn."

"Thanks. I wish I had more than a sketchy general knowledge myself. At my gallery all those years ago I'm afraid we only specialised in local talent."

"Mr Carrington always says the wish is the deed. I came here six years ago totally ignorant about art of any kind, but I wanted to learn and I have." Sonia smiled in triumph, but her forehead glistened with sweat and Phyllida could still hear her breathing.

"The Pre-Raphaelites have always fascinated me," Anita told her. "They're so English. I've meant to read up about them, but somehow. . . . That's how life is, isn't it?"

"Unless you get the opportunity you've got now. David Lester's your man, he's our expert on the Pre-Raphaelites. There's special excitement in that department at the

40

moment because of the two Frederick Sandys turning up last year. You'll have heard about them?" Anita nodded. Best to be honest where she could, and a little knowledge wouldn't stand in the way of acquiring more. "Sandys had said he was going to paint them, but nobody knew he'd actually got round to it, not even David." Sonia's excitedly helpless expression probably reflected the reactions of the rest of the Snaith Gallery staff. "They just came in the post. Anonymously." She gave Mrs Sunbury a sudden keen look. "Nothing to do with you, Mrs Sunbury? A Getty gesture?"

Mrs Sunbury laughed, then looked wistful. "I only wish it were, honey. I don't have Getty money. Or access to national treasures. What an excitement, though! I suppose the pictures had to go through a whole range of processes before they were accepted as the genuine article?"

"Oh, yes."

"And you haven't had any more?"

"No!" The vehemence of Sonia's denial was at odds with the uncertainty in her face. But Peter had warned her that *Winter* was still classified. "There could only be one more, anyway," Sonia went on quickly, "because of them representing the four seasons. David was over the moon."

Phyllida wondered if her use of the past tense had any significance. In the gallery as well as at home, David Lester's current and obvious state of mind was not elation. "He doesn't show it, does he? In fact he struck me as – well. . . . the type of a chronic worrier. Oh, that sounds ridiculous, and anyway I don't know him."

"No." Sonia now was thoughtful. "But you're right, David hasn't looked too happy lately. Which isn't him at all. Maybe when . . ." She tailed off, and Phyllida saw a shutter come down over the frank brown eyes.

"Yes?"

"I'm sorry," Sonia said. All her weight now was on

the desk. "I need to flop. If you feel I told you enough yesterday afternoon to enable you to face the crowds on your own."

"You did, honey. You go off home now."

Sonia waddled off and Phyllida drew the chair she had vacated close to the desk, felt a pang of regret at the ease of the movement and its reminder that she was unlikely now ever to experience Sonia's current discomforts. Gerald, her husband, had never identified a time suitable for having children. . . .

It all appeared very leisurely, Phyllida thought, as she looked round the quiet space and forced her mind to follow her eyes. There were a few browsers and possibly clients moving gently about the main gallery, mostly alone but two in earnest *sotto voce* conversation with members of staff, and people had walked in and out of the smaller galleries while she and Sonia were talking, but the surface pace was definitely *andante legato*, soothingly out of tune with her own adrenalin-pumping tempo.

She had answered a number of simple queries, and directed a couple of people to specific areas with only one glance at the notes she had made, when she saw Philip Morgan escort a client to the door. As he turned, saw her, and came across to her, Phyllida realised she had been anticipating the moment.

"Mrs Sunbury! How are you getting on?"

"I'm enjoying myself, if that's an answer."

"Oh, it is." He leaned against the desk. "People don't enjoy themselves enough these days. Or if they do, they don't let it show. Isn't that true?"

"Perhaps." Phyllida thought of one or two people considerably younger than herself who never admitted to excitement or enthusiasm.

"I think it is. Is there any way I can help you?"

Alone with her for the first time, he was trying to tone down his interest and admiration, but they remained

42

palpable. Steve at the Agency was making a bit of a fool of himself over Mrs Sunbury, and one or two of Phyllida's earlier incarnations had evoked admiration, but never with such potential strength as this. And never with so strong an instinct in herself to respond, all the stronger because since the beginnings of her marriage break-up she had thought the instinct was dead. Again she forced herself to remember that it was not Phyllida Moon Philip Morgan was finding attractive.

Anita returned his smile. "Not at the moment, thanks," she said, and Phyllida reprimanded her for gratuitous provocation. "Sonia's been splendid," she amended. "She gave me the general idea in just one afternoon."

"One could say it was splendid to pick up the general idea in just one afternoon. I gather you once had a gallery of your own?"

"Oh – that!" Having made use of it, Mrs Sunbury would now shrug it off with becoming modesty. "That was years ago and just for local talent, no national or international treasures. But it was fun, I enjoyed making my small space as attractive as possible and being in charge of it."

"So why have you taken so long to come back to it?"

"One thing and another." She was glad to see that the couple who had just come through the door were approaching the desk.

"Perhaps you'll tell me about them over a drink this evening? Say in the Connaught round about six? Or perhaps the Golden Lion?"

The couple were waiting. And Anita Sunbury wasn't the sort of woman who floundered. "Not the Golden Lion. I'll meet you in the Connaught." At least there was no need to agonise over her response. Accepting every opportunity short of the life-threatening or the obscene was part of her brief.

43

"Good." Philip Morgan strolled away, and Phyllida turned her attention with relief to her clients.

Despite the leisurely surface pace of life behind the double glass doors of the Snaith Gallery the time went quickly. By the time Deborah appeared, Anita had satisfied about a dozen customers, half of whom – both men and women – had been disposed to linger chatting beside the desk. It was ten past three, and Deborah, wreathed in plastic shopping bags, was breathlessly apologetic.

"It was the queue at the check-out, and the girl in front of me couldn't find her purse. . . ."

"That's all right, honey, I've been enjoying myself. But when you've sorted yourself out I'll be glad for you to sit here a bit so that I can have another look around."

Anita was studying a small late Turner when a more rapid step than she had heard that afternoon stopped beside her.

"Ah. Mrs Sunbury. How are you getting on?"

Phyllida turned to face Pamela Bennett. Close to and undiluted by the presence of unfamiliar people, she struck Phyllida as even more combative than she had appeared the day before.

"Thank you, everyone has been so helpful."

"Mm. Know much about pictures?"

"Not as much as I'd like to."

"What everyone says."

"I mean it, honey."

"Then learn. There's no law against it."

And no sense of humour, Phyllida suspected, behind those scornful eyes.

"I'm hoping to. I think this is your life, isn't it, Miss Bennett?" Mrs Sunbury gently suggested. "I think you're pretty single-minded?"

Pamela Bennett blinked, taken aback by even so mild a counter-attack. "Of course!" she snapped.

"And ambitious?"

"Of course!" Miss Bennett repeated irritably. "Ah, David!"

Phyllida could have fallen on Miss Bennett's scrawny neck as what Steve would have called her subject reluctantly approached in response to the summons.

"Yes, Pam?"

"Any word yet about the you know what? When do we expect the verdict?"

Whatever else he might be, David Lester was not an actor. His body sagged and he moistened his lips before his whispered "By the end of the week". Phyllida turned quickly to look at Miss Bennett. David Lester had reacted so dramatically to her coded question that even someone as self-absorbed as Pamela Bennett must surely react in her turn.

But Miss Bennett appeared as fierce and impersonal as ever, and Phyllida wondered if she saw pictures at the expense of seeing people. "You've been very fortunate," she pronounced sternly to Mrs Sunbury. Professional sour grapes, or a twist by the torturer of the rack on which her victim lay?

It was all too easy to see Pamela Bennett in the role of the torturer, and she must resist the temptation.

But David Lester had put out his hand for the support of the wall.

Chapter Four

The single window in the Snaith Gallery staff room, or rest room as it was referred to, looked on to a view closely resembling the prospect from Phyllida's sanctum at the Golden Lion – an internal well – and Thelma Royle was drawing a heavy brown curtain against it as Mrs Sunbury walked in through the open doorway at just after four o'clock. By the time Anita reached the teapot Thelma had diffused the overhead light beam by switching on a couple of lamps that stood on low tables, and the place had assumed quite a cosy look.

"This is a winter room," Thelma greeted Anita. "There's never much daylight, but in the summer you feel you ought to try and make do with what there is. The tea's fresh, but you can always make some if it isn't on the go. How're you getting on?" She puffed her way towards an armchair almost as awkwardly as Sonia must have taken possession of the one in which Phyllida was surprised to see her sprawling.

"I'm enjoying myself," Anita repeated. "Though I still can't quite believe I'm here."

"I'm glad you are," Thelma said, stretching her short legs. "Sonia's had enough."

"For the time being." Sonia was relaxed and smiling, the qualification was a reflex.

"So how come you're still here, honey? I saw you leave."

"But not come back, you were too busy. I went

46

shopping, and then I was suddenly dying for some tea." Sonia burst out laughing. "It's really relaxing here now, thanks to you and Miss- what's the morning lady called, Thelma?"

"Sheila Burns."

Sonia pulled a face. "You'll keep her in her place, won't you, Thelma?" She yawned, smiling at Anita.

"I shall, you mustn't worry. And I'll keep your memory green with Mr Carrington."

"You make it sound like I'm going to die instead of have a baby," Sonia protested. But it was already obvious to Phyllida that these two were old sparring partners.

"Does everyone come in here for tea and coffee?" Anita asked as she sat down.

"From Mr Brooke to the porters if they feel like it, but I take Mr Carrington his in his office. Mr Brooke and David and Philip and Pam sometimes take theirs back to their cells."

"Their cells?"

"You can't quite call them offices," Sonia took over lazily. "They're just recesses in the walls with enough room for a desk, two chairs and a filing cabinet."

"You'll have seen the experts behind their desks staring hopefully out for custom," Thelma said.

"Read 'angrily' so far as Pam's concerned," Sonia resumed. "Mr Carrington likes their doors to be kept open while the gallery's open so they can always see and be seen, but I sometimes wonder if he's afraid they'll suffocate if they close them. Hello, Mr Brooke. Meet Mrs Sunbury. She started yesterday when you were in London. She's taken over from me pro tem in the afternoons."

"Indeed, Sonia? I hope all goes well for you. Good afternoon, Mrs Sunbury."

"Good afternoon, Mr Brooke." The man whose special-isation was Victorian genre painting was tall and frail

47

and clearly approaching his official retirement date. Phyllida's immediate impression was of genuine and unaffected refinement, from the barely fleshed face to the pale long-fingered hands and soft voice. The eyes were noticeably blue and intelligent.

"Mrs Sunbury." Phyllida was glad he took her hand, she had wanted to touch one of his in the moment of seeing them. "I hope you'll be happy here." The hand was cold.

"Thank you."

"You're looking demure," Mr Brooke said. "But you're not."

"He's devastating," Sonia said. "I was about to warn you."

Thelma looked at her watch, then scrambled to her feet. "Mr Carrington should be through with his client. I'd better get back, he's off to London tonight."

"I shall sit here," Sonia purred, "for the rest of the afternoon."

"You do that, honey. I'll get back too." Anita drained her coffee cup, and Phyllida hoped she might escape before Philip Morgan appeared – she had done her duty by him until the date she had secured. He had secured. But however it had come her way, she must make professional use of it.

She went next door into the staff cloakroom, where there was a payphone in an enclave, and dialled the agency. Although her voice was muffled by surrounding coats and mackintoshes, it was Anita who drawled Phyllida's disappointment to Jenny that she was going to be tied up after work and wouldn't be able to make it that evening. "So don't any of you wait for me, honey, I'll see you in the morning." Peter she might see that night, if there was a light in his office window when she got back to the Golden Lion.

"Okay, Mrs Sunbury. Tomorrow it will have to be,

48

then." Jenny's voice was amused and disappointed at the same time, and Phyllida thought she heard Steve wail in the background.

On her way back to the reception desk she passed Pam Bennett's cell – she would never be able to call the small offices anything else to herself, having heard Thelma's definition – and was surprised at the expression on her face as she stood absorbed with a sketch in her hands: respectful, even loving. Perhaps she had been right in wondering if Miss Bennett preferred pictures to people. Or, at the least, was impatient with people because they failed to appreciate pictures as they should, even her fellow experts. Sensing a pausing presence, as she and her other cellmates must have learned to, Miss Bennett looked up, and Phyllida found the restoration of her face to its usual irritability as sad as it was dramatic. Nodding and half smiling, Anita Sunbury walked on.

She must also pass David Lester's cell to reach the main gallery and he was in it, rummaging through a filing drawer without watching his fingers, then, as she paused, leaning forward to butt his head several times against the top edge of the cabinet. He too sensed a presence, and when he turned to look out through his doorway his eyes were as fearful as Phyllida had seen them when he had spoken to Mrs Cookson about answering the telephone.

He was instantly smiling, but Mrs Sunbury apologised. "I'm sorry, I guess I must have looked awfully nosy. But I'm just trying to find out what there is here."

"Of course. Nothing much in this corner, I'm afraid." Phyllida reflected with an inward smile that David Lester was likely to be the only man in Seaminster whose reactions to Mrs Cookson and Mrs Sunbury were precisely the same.

Mrs Sunbury took a step towards his sanctum. "But you're the Pre-Raphaelite specialist, aren't you, Mr

49

Lester? I read about the Frederick Sandys discoveries, they must have been really exciting for you."

She'd seen this expression on his face before, too. When Mrs Cookson had admired the gallery windows. "They were, yes." But David Lester looked as though he wished he had never set eyes on them. "When I learned they were the real thing it felt like a miracle." He was making an effort, and Phyllida imagined sadly how the words he was using must have sounded the day before he received the first anonymous letter. *Why* had it had so profound an effect on him? And *why* hadn't he done what his sister had expected him to do: gone to the police?

"I've always been interested in the Pre-Raphaelites, as people as well as painters."

David Lester was back at his files. "They're marvellously well documented. Even some of the peripheral characters, like Sandys." He pulled out a folder. "There was a Sandys exhibition in Brighton in 1974, and he was included with a good biographical detail in an exhibition of Pre-Raphaelite painting at the Tate ten years later. I've only got one precious catalogue of each, but if you're really interested I'll get them photostatted for you."

"I really am, and I'd love to have them. Thank you. You're very kind." She could imagine he had been, before his worries had overwhelmed him. The folder in his hand brought her another pang, as evidence of a vanished dedication. It was an effort to remind herself that the man attempting to smile at her could be a cheat and a thief.

Phyllida was glad Philip Morgan hadn't suggested they left the gallery together, although she wondered if it could be because he had a reputation for making up to temps and didn't want his colleagues to tease him about yet another conquest. Dismissing the speculation as

50

unprofessional, she watched how Deborah closed down the reception desk.

"You'll never have to set it up," Deborah said wistfully. "It's a shame you can't come all day."

"Never mind, Deborah. I expect Ms Burns will turn out just fine."

Philip Morgan was awaiting Mrs Sunbury in the remotest corner of the Connaught's cocktail lounge, and Phyllida smiled to herself as she approached it because it was the corner where she had met Peter in her first incarnation as Anita Sunbury and ended up being hired by him as Phyllida Moon. As he had once said, the Golden Lion was the most exclusive of Seaminster's hotels, but the Connaught was the smartest and most showy. It was only just after six o'clock, but already the place was buzzing with expensive-looking visitors and sharply dressed businessmen discussing deals over shorts. Anita Sunbury graced the Connaught almost as aptly as she graced the Golden Lion, and Philip Morgan, in the smart suit that was a little too light in colour for Phyllida's taste, looked more like a wealthy businessman than an art expert.

"How nice, Anita. What would you like to drink?"

"Gin and dry martini?"

A waiter was already hovering, as one always would be when Anita Sunbury appeared in a bar. Had Philip Morgan been sitting with Phyllida Moon he would probably still be trying to catch the man's eye. But Phyllida would have been able to discourage Philip's personal interest – in the unlikely event of his showing any – without any trouble, whereas that particular ability was not high among Anita Sunbury's talents. But there were always fictions to fall back on, which would be no more than extensions of the big fiction that was Mrs Sunbury herself. . . .

The dry martinis came in Art Deco-style funnels with black stems, and contained speared green olives.

51

"So," Mrs Sunbury said, having taken a sip and set her glass down. "Your specialty is modern art, Philip?"

"Modern art in comparison with the specialities of the other gallery staff would probably be the most accurate way to describe it. The gallery only opened its doors to the moderns a few years ago, and we've never shown anything really wild or aggressive. But a pickled ewe or a continuous video of male buttocks in the main gallery is pretty unimaginable."

"Yes. Perhaps it's time to recognise a new talent, under the heading of ingenuity. Literature, music, art, and ingenuity." They both laughed, but Phyllida knew that it was time to get down to work. "The girls have been telling me about the Sandys finds. It's amazing, isn't it? I think I remember hearing about them on the news."

"You would have done, there was a lot of excitement."

"What do you make of it? I mean, why the anonymity? Why on earth should anyone who had such a potential goldmine not dig it for himself?"

"That's the big question we're all asking. At first we thought it must be because the pictures were fakes, but when they were authenticated there was no way we could understand whoever had handed them to us."

"Unless they were stolen – maybe generations ago – and someone wanted to make amends."

"Yes." He threw her an admiring glance which Phyllida's professional self welcomed as being for the mind rather than the body. If she could keep the expert talk going through the inevitable second drink she might be able to keep the fictions for another time. "But that would still involve altruism to an incredible degree. The same again?"

The waiter was back. Anita nodded. "Thanks. The gallery's the beneficiary, then," she said thoughtfully.

"Perhaps it's someone's way of supporting it. Is Mr Carrington the sole owner?"

"Yes. He started with a partner 15 years or so ago, but he died soon after. He's talked to his widow and daughter, of course, since the pictures started arriving, but they've convinced him, and everyone else, that they know nothing about them."

The waiter set the second drinks in front of them. "There's no one else to benefit, then?" Mrs Sunbury asked innocently.

"Well. . . ." Philip Morgan looked uncomfortable. "David Lester's our expert on the Pre-Raphaelites, as you probably know by now. And believe me, he really is. And he's the one who's earned the commissions on the sale of the two pictures authenticated so far. When the first one came and he was so enthusiastic about it, so sure it was genuine, there was a bit of talk . . . but when it got the all clear. . . . Even if David had anything to do with sending the pictures," Philip said, looking exasperated by his own bewilderment, "he isn't benefiting from it beyond getting fairly earned commissions for selling authenticated works of art. And he seemed so genuinely staggered when he saw the first picture. As well as wildly excited."

"He didn't seem wildly excited today."

"No." His faced showed the suddenly thoughtful look Phyllida was getting used to seeing when she commented on David Lester's reactions a week or so ago and his reactions now. "No," Philip Morgan repeated. "He isn't. He's anything but, now you mention it. He hasn't been his usual quietly cheerful self since – oh, I don't know, a week or so? I've noticed it without registering it, if you know what I mean. Perhaps he's got troubles at home."

"Has he got a family?"

"Just a sister, who he lives with. I gather there was

a wife, but they were divorced years ago. No children. That's hearsay, by the way, I've never spoken to him about anything except gallery business."

"It's intriguing, you know." Mrs Sunbury was taking her second drink more slowly than her first. "The wonderful discoveries, the expert's elation, then suddenly – his chin's on the floor. Why? It's the stuff of crime fiction."

"But there's no crime!"

"No. . . . And no more pictures?"

She saw the lie he must have told so often come into his face, but under her steady gaze it dissolved in a laugh. "Yes," he said. "Yes! *Winter* arrived a week or so ago and is currently undergoing the tests. Which I'm under oath not to tell you. When *Spring* arrived and David thought it was all right, Mr Carrington made us all promise to keep quiet about it unless and until it was authenticated. So that if it turned out to be a fake no one beyond the gallery staff and the expert would know it existed. Keeping quiet's become more important with each picture, as you'll appreciate. Once the media were in on the miracle – which they were, of course, the moment *Spring* got the OK – secrecy over subsequent pictures really became vital. If the outside world knew a picture had been declared a dud, doubt would be cast over the whole series. And *Spring* and *Summer* have been sold."

"You're very trusting," Anita observed. "I could be a media person."

"Yes," he agreed, smiling at her. "I've realised that while I've been breaking my oath. Not just because it's the sort of thing a suspicious news editor might set up. I had a mad idea when you asked me if there was a third picture that you already knew there was." Anita shook her head, smiling, and he sighed. "That's one reason it was so easy. The other . . . just you, I'm afraid." The rueful look again, the helpless spread of the hands. For the first time Phyllida found herself attracted to Philip Morgan the person as well as Philip Morgan the man. "I'm at your mercy," he said.

"I'm not a media person, honey, and I won't get you into trouble. But haven't you got your answer to David Lester's misery? He's sold and earned commissions on two historic goldmines that could finally turn out to be just two holes in the ground. He's bound to be sweating blood. For the third time! I guess he's in need of a transfusion."

"You're right, as I'm sure you very often are. Once we have the good news on *Winter* he'll be himself again. At least we know there can't be a fourth picture, there being only four seasons of the year. Now. . . ." Philip Morgan leaned towards her, and Phyllida saw his expression change as his eyes ceased to see Mrs Sunbury's head as a brainbox. She hadn't asked him to break his promise, but he must have hope of a reward. She thought gratefully of the small room at the Golden Lion, where Anita Sunbury could be humanely despatched. "Perhaps we could talk a little about ourselves? How about moving into the restaurant and having—"

"I'm so sorry," Anita said. "I have to be—" She glanced at her watch and gave an exclamation of surprise. "Time's gone so quickly! I'm supposed to be at a friend's house at seven-fifteen, and it's almost that already. I really must go, forgive me."

"That's a pity." She had to hide her disappointment, but Philip Morgan could show his. "I'll forgive you, though, if you'll promise to have dinner with me another time. You will?"

"We'll see." She had to keep the initiative, however strong her unfamiliar desire to lose it. "Thank you for tonight, anyway, I've enjoyed it."

"So have I. I'm afraid I haven't got my car, but can I

walk you anywhere?" *And find out where you're going and what sort of place it is.*

"Thanks, but I have to call in at my hotel first." Philip Morgan's question, and others like it, were the reason Peter had devised her the safety net of the Golden Lion. Where she would shed Mrs Sunbury and then walk home by the dark sea to spend a few hours in her beloved and neglected house before driving back to the Golden Lion for the night. . . .

"Okay. I'll walk you that far. All right?

"Of course."

He took her arm and she didn't pull it free, which would have been churlish. Whatever else she did or didn't do, she must not turn this man into an enemy. And equally must not, she realized with a pang of mingled reassurance and dismay as they stood gravely facing one another on the steps of the Golden Lion, allow physical contact to reveal the physical unreality of Anita Sunbury.

Phyllida was glad to get home, and it was an effort to leave again just at the point when she was ready to change into a dressing-gown and bedroom slippers and pour herself a whisky. But it was compensation to get into her car for once in the way of business, and tuck it in behind the Golden Lion. She entered the hotel the back way, and went straight through the foyer and out of the main door to look at the office of Peter Piper Private Investigator on the other side of the square.

Two of the sash windows were alight, the one nearer Peter's desk the brighter.

Phyllida crossed the square via an obtuse angle of pathway, unlocked the outer doors of Number 36, climbed the two flights of stairs, and let herself into the agency. Peter's "Come in!" from behind his office door was unsurprised.

"I'm glad you're still here," she said as she flopped

down in the armchair facing his desk. "I'm an owl too, you know, and it's frustrating having to wait till next day to talk. Especially now there's no time to come in at lunchtime and at least report on the morning."

"So, lots to talk about tonight?"

"Yes."

"Good." Peter gestured towards his drinks cabinet, and she nodded. "Good," he said again as he opened it. "Fire away."

She had made notes on the day during her short time at home but she spoke without them, telling him everything she could think of apart from her own inward response to Philip Morgan's interest in Anita Sunbury.

"That was always a danger with Anita," Peter said. "I mean, if *Steve*. . . ."

"*You* had more sense." One of the bonuses between herself and Peter was that they had been instant brother and sister.

"Ah, well." He was unembarrassed. "I had other things. . . . And although I may not look like one I'm a realist, I could see she was beyond my personal grasp. And I do feel awfully business-minded about the agency. It was Mrs Sunbury's custom I lusted after. Attractive, is he? This Philip Morgan?" Peter asked, with apparently innocent curiosity.

"I suppose so, now I think about it. He's certainly not unattractive." Phyllida hoped this was the only time she would find herself deceiving Peter, it was an uncomfortable experience. But there was no need to alarm him over something which would never become alarming. "I saw to it that we only talked business, and I got my reward."

"Quite a sizeable one," Peter commented, his eyes on her face. "Are there likely to be problems?"

"Yes, I'll have to bring out some fictions. About not being ready because of not being over my husband's death, or something. Anita's too phoney to stand up to much, anyway. One thing about sleuthing in character, Peter, it keeps a detective on the straight and narrow." With an effort, Phyllida laughed.

"I didn't think about that."

"Don't think about it now, there's no need."

"Right." He was still studying her face. "So you didn't get the feeling Philip Morgan had written the letters. Any feelings about anyone else?"

If his choice of words was more than coincidence, she was sure he was unaware of it. "It's all too easy to see Pamela Bennett as the villain of any piece. On the other hand, anonymous letter writing is a sneaky sort of an occupation, and Ms Bennett makes no secret of her contempt for the human race."

"Inconsistent, if you think about it, seeing that the human race is responsible for her beloved works of art."

"Yes! Mrs Sunbury might put that proposition to her, her response would be interesting. There's nothing I can say to you about anyone else, I'm afraid, but they all seem so bright its hardly likely the letter writer will be careless or stupid enough to give him or herself away."

"But judgment is about to be delivered on *Winter*, which is the picture the letters have told David Lester to look out for, and you'll be on the spot if it turns out to be a fake. Even the brightest culprit may not be able to prevent some reaction at that point, and anyway he or she won't know they're under a spotlight glowing unseen inside the new receptionist. You'll be there, Phyllida, able to look closely at all of them."

"Unless the news breaks in the morning, and whoever it is has had time to get his or her glee under control by the afternoon."

"Don't tell me they'll have managed to do *that* by lunchtime. You'll still be in a unique position. And

58

the whole thing about an art gallery is that people are expected to be wandering about, looking. If you think you've been spotted looking in the wrong direction, there's always a convenient picture nearby you can pretend to have been studying all the time."

"And there's always the possibility that the letter writer doesn't work at the gallery," Phyllida contributed, smiling.

"In which case a little more may happen at The Cedars than happened yesterday," Peter encouraged.

Phyllida laughed. "Don't worry, Peter, I don't need jollying. I'm not frustrated, I'm having the time of my life."

Chapter Five

The rough circle of ground at the end of the lane off Marlborough Drive was still deserted when Phyllida nosed her car into it next morning, and she parked and got out quickly. Mrs Cookson looked so unlikely to be in charge of a vehicle she was anxious to distance herself from it as rapidly as possible, and crossed the circle at a crouched run.

Towards the mouth of the lane she slowed to Mrs Cookson's usual brisk trot. It was a calm, crisp morning, the unshaded parts of the frosted lawns she passed already greening under the brilliance of a sun which shone directly into her eyes and had her almost colliding with the taxi emerging from a gateway.

The gateway to The Cedars.

Through the dazzle Phyllida had a blurry glimpse of a female face looking fearfully towards her. She blessed a passing car for making the taxi wait, but by the time her eyes had adjusted to the brilliance the face was a profile – motionless, taut, and intriguingly beautiful.

When the taxi swung out into the road and headed towards town, Phyllida went in through The Cedar's gates without pausing to watch it go, on an instinct to avert the danger of putting the woman on an alert which would have her telephoning David Lester and suggesting the curtailing of some activity which if it continued might yield some information. . . .

Phyllida was concentrating on her thoughts, and the

front door ahead of her, and didn't see the shabby little man who always asked people to call him Barney freeze among the thick bushes on one side of the forecourt as she crossed it. When she was admitted to the house and the door had closed again, he continued his cautious progress to the gate, where he quickly sidled out and turned right along Marlborough Drive towards the side street where he had parked his car. On his way he passed the narrow lane, peered up it, and saw Phyllida's. It hadn't been there when he arrived and it was when he had his notebook out to record its number that he made the bizarre connection with the Hilda Ogden lookalike he had just seen on its way into The Cedars. So he smiled at the car instead, shaking his head as he walked on and reflected on the dramatic rise of the lower classes.

"That has to be the clincher," he said aloud as he got into his own car and threw the notebook down on the stained and sagging seat beside him. "So now for the pay off, Barney my boy." He felt like an immediate celebration, but there was nothing to drink in the car, and nothing edible apart from half a bag of stale potato crisps. He ate them staring out of the window, enjoying the rare sensation of the smile that was still on his face.

Wiping her feet on the inside mat, Mrs Cookson smiled at David Lester.

"Good morning, Mr Lester, lovely morning, innit?"

"I suppose so." Her employer peered past her as she entered the house, his expression as fearful as the expression on the face she had just seen. A face which in her memory was a fearful expression and nothing else, Phyllida thought regretfully.

But she had at least learned that a beautiful woman had called on David Lester, and at an unsocial hour. And that her visit had left him, this second morning of Mrs Cookson's ministrations, in physical as well as mental disarray. His hair was uncombed (tousled by female fingers?), and he had yet to put on jacket or tie. Phyllida was also aware of a rosy fulness about his lips which had been absent the morning before and in the gallery, and which she recalled on an involuntary shudder having seen around Gerald's mouth in the old days after they'd been. . . .

"Makes you think about spring, dunnit, a morning like this, Mr Lester?"

David Lester had been looking from Mrs Cookson to the gate, and from the gate to Mrs Cookson, and had now evidently decided in the light of her direct entry to the cloakroom to hang her coat and put on her overall, her prattle and her incurious air, that she had either not seen or not registered the departing cab.

Phyllida saw him relax. "Yes, it does, doesn't it? Beautiful morning. . . . Frozen fish tonight, Mrs Cookson. It's a packet thing with mashed potato on top, so I'll only need carrots, if you'll be so good."

"Yes, I'll do that, Mr Lester." Mrs Cookson followed her employer into the kitchen, talking all the time and deliberately not noticing him pick up one of the two mugs on the table and slip it in among the few pots soaking in the sink. So it must have contained coffee dregs, like the one that still stood there. "Carrots are all right, aren't they, I'm all for carrots. You don't want to be eating that junk food every night, you know, Mr Lester, it's got no nourishment."

He had relaxed again, was pouring coffee into the remaining mug. "I had fresh chicken last night, Mrs Cookson, as you of all people know. And my sister is only away until Saturday. I think I'll survive."

"Yes, well . . ." Mrs Cookson conceded.

"Everything all right yesterday? No telephone calls?"

"Not one, Mr Lester. And the house like a new pin before I got a duster out."

"I told you, didn't I?" He was actually grinning. But

62

Phyllida was aware of an exhilaration in him which there had been no sign of the day before, at home or at work. A sense that there might, after all, be some hope.

A hope the profile she had glimpsed in the car had been lacking.

"You did, yes, Mr Lester. Perhaps you'll 'ave done me a good turn this morning, and left an 'air or two on the wash basin."

Mrs Cookson laughed heartily at her own joke, watching David Lester sustain a shock before forcing himself to join in. Afraid that, if there were any hairs, they might be noticeably longer than his?

"It's time I wasn't here." He was abruptly sombre.

"Yes, o'course, 'ere's me talking too much as usual. Off you go now and 'ave a nice day, as them Yanks put it."

Yesterday he would scarcely have heard her, but this morning he was aware enough to wince, and he turned with a final smile in the kitchen doorway.

As the sound of the car died away, Phyllida went to the sink. The arc of lipstick on the edge of the mug just added to the slimy water was confirmation of what she already knew, but it yielded the additional information that David Lester's visitor made her face up before breakfast. If there was nothing else to report by the end of the week, Phyllida reflected ruefully, Mrs Everett would at least know that Peter Piper Private Investigator paid attention to detail. . . .

The one letter addressed to David Lester which he had left on the kitchen table was a bill for plumbing, but Phyllida had at least some food for thought and some hope of further revelation as she went back into the hall. Her employer *was* taking advantage of his sister's absence, the departing taxi was evidence enough of that, and his sleight of hand with the mug showed that he wanted to keep his visitor a secret. But was the woman with the anguished profile to do with his business or his private life? If she hadn't known David Lester's recent history, Phyllida's instincts in the light of the reactions of both parties would have inclined her towards passion rather than sharp practice, but it was an unlikely coincidence that he should have two guilty secrets.

There would be no answers to her question without further discovery, and there were none supplied by her quick survey of the ground floor. Phyllida was halfway up the stairs when the letterbox snapped, and almost fell down them in her eagerness to investigate the post.

One manilla envelope, addressed to David Lester. But again there was print behind a window and the flap was tucked in: a receipt for payment received for work carried out on one motor-powered lawn-mower.

Phyllida put it on the kitchen dresser beside the letters already there for Mrs Everett and went back up the stairs. The guest bedroom looked precisely as she had left it the day before, and there was no scent from the wardrobe to dilute the camphor. In the small en-suite bathroom there was no drop of water, no dampness even, and the ends of the loo paper still hung in the point into which Mrs Cookson had pressed them twenty-four hours earlier – a variant on the hair-across-the-lock test and a small piece of negative evidence for her report.

She would keep Mrs Everett's room till last – whatever the state of his morale, her brother would surely not accommodate a guest there – and, heart pumping as she reached her last hope of apocalypse, Phyllida entered David Lester's.

A quick glance round offered no evidence of anything different from the way it had been the morning before and she went across to the bathroom, jerking to attention when she was still in the doorway.

Nothing to be seen, but a message for her nose. Scent. Scent totally, unambiguously feminine. Not that it needed

64

to be unambiguous: the morning before there had been no scent of a masculine kind. And there was no aftershave in the medicine chest or on the glass shelves.

The bathroom was as neat and clean as it had been yesterday, the basin and bath as hairless, but in the linen basket there was a hand towel with face powder on it. The waste-paper basket in the bedroom was empty, but when she drew back the duvet cover on the small double bed Phyllida found the scent on the pillow.

Well satisfied, she turned to face the rest of the room, and the object on the chest of drawers winked at her as if there was a lighted bulb at its heart.

She ran over to take it into her hand. A gold bracelet set with opals and pearls to form daisy-shape flowers, intricately delicate in the surprising way of Victorian jewellery in the light of Victorian furniture. Phyllida chided herself for her thought that it matched the beautiful profile. Wishful thinking had no part in her brief.

She put on her surgical gloves as she went into Mrs Everett's bedroom. When she had looked round and found nothing changed, she carefully opened dressing-table drawers until she found a jewel box. When she took it out and poked about in it she found only bold modern pieces of the type Mrs Everett had been wearing when she interviewed Mrs Cookson. Another piece of negative evidence, if not one for Peter to include in his report.

Phyllida returned the bracelet to the chest of drawers before making a more detailed survey of David Lester's bedroom. She had no conscience about neglecting her cleaning duties that morning, and when she was sure there was nothing else to discover she went back to the kitchen to make herself coffee, poking her duster in token acknowledgement of her job description into the intricacies of the Art Nouveau banisters – the only avant-garde feature of the Edwardian house – on her way downstairs.

She took the coffee to the kitchen table, sat down, and produced the small notebook from her apron pocket. But instead of writing she sat in thought, question marks abounding in her brain. She had established that David Lester's visitor had been there for his pleasure, but was he combining the pleasure with illicit business? If not, then it must be the woman herself who was illicit. Another man's wife? A prostitute?

And did the agency report the liaison to David Lester's sister?

That was for Peter to decide when he had read her report, and Phyllida at last put pen to paper. When the telephone rang her pen traced a wavering line down the rest of the page, and she decided as she ran into the hall that the arrival of what she awaited, in hope or in dread, was a greater shock than the arrival of the unexpected.

"Hello?"

"Who is that?" A male voice, on alert.

"Who is *that*, please?" Not telephone protocol, but Mrs Cookson's was likely to be shaky, and her counter-question offered the only possibility of identifying the caller.

"I want to speak to Mr Jones," the voice said, exasperated.

"I'm afraid there's no Mr Jones 'ere. And Mrs Everett and Mr Lester—"

"I've obviously got the wrong number. I'm sorry to have troubled you."

"That's all right. . . ." But the other receiver had gone down.

Phyllida went thoughtfully back into the kitchen, the telephone call giving place to the implications of the bracelet as she picked up her pen. As soon as David Lester saw it that night it would begin to burn a hole in his chest of drawers and one way or another he would have to get it back to the profile. . . .

She heard the key in the lock as she was deciding she had written all she could. When David Lester came into the kitchen carrying a briefcase Mrs Cookson was pouring bleach down the sink.

"'ello!" she said. "I wasn't expecting to see *you* again today! Everything all right? Can I make you a coffee?"

"Everything's fine, Mrs Cookson. Thank you, but I don't have time for coffee. I've just come to pick up some papers I need for a meeting. One thing about living and working in a small town, it's easy travelling between your home and your office." He paused, looking past her. "Did you find any hairs in the bathroom?" The jokiness in his voice was tremulous.

"No, Mr Lester, but that's because I ain't been upstairs yet, I've started downstairs today. Nothing like variety, is there?"

"That's true enough." His relieved laughter was inordinate. "Right, then. I'll just pick up what I need."

"One letter for you come by the second post." Mrs Cookson nodded towards the dresser and Phyllida saw the violent start followed by the deliberate casualness with which David Lester approached the dresser. And the trembling of his hand as he picked up the manilla envelope.

"Just a receipt." He had had difficulty opening the envelope.

"Better than a bill, eh?" Mrs Cookson suggested.

"Much better." David Lester forced a smile, and left the kitchen. Phyllida heard his feet immediately on the stairs, and less than a minute had passed when he reappeared and told her he was off.

"I almost forgot," Mrs Cookson said, pursuing him into the hall. "'alf an hour or so ago there was a telephone call. A man asking for Mr Jones." She paused to note another shock, and observed another attempt to hide it. So there had been anonymous phone calls, too. "Wrong number, o'course. But the way 'e banged the phone down, you'd of thought it was *my* fault."

"That was quite unnecessary," David Lester struggled. "I've had a few of these – wrong numbers – lately. What – what was the voice like, Mrs Cookson?"

Mrs Cookson shrugged. "Couldn't say, reelly. I mean, I didn't 'ardly 'ear enough of it. Posh, if anythink."

"Thanks. Well, I'll be off. See you in the morning."

"See you in the morning."

See you this afternoon, Phyllida amended aloud as the front door banged, then howled her frustration at her distance from her car. If it had been in the drive she would have followed him on his beeline to return the bracelet. She was so sure he had come home to collect it she had another coffee before going back upstairs to check.

"You can feel it, can't you?" Philip Morgan said. "The tension."

"Yes," Anita murmured. This afternoon she had been unable to avoid taking her tea break at the time Philip took his. He had noted her passage past his cell and had arrived in the staff rest room a few moments later, appearing to amble without aim to the arm of the chair where she was sitting. David Lester had just poured himself tea and gone off with it. Remaining in the room while they drank theirs were Mr Brooke and Pamela Bennett, Pamela at least so absorbed in argument she seemed scarcely aware of Mrs Sunbury and Mr Morgan. Watching the increasing polarisation of the other pair – Mr Brooke growing quieter and more deliberate as Miss Bennett grew noisier and more vehement – Phyllida reflected with amusement that even among a team of TV sitcom writers so obvious a contrast would have been judged too crudely simplistic.

"After our conversation last night you know why." Philip hardly bothered to lower his voice, but Phyllida

68

suspected Mr Brooke of being aware of them, and of their proximity to one another.

"Awaiting the verdict on *Winter*." Mrs Sunbury had lowered hers.

"That's it."

"When will it come?" She wasn't looking at him, she was looking across at the other two and trying to discover what their argument was about. When she caught the words "artistic integrity" from Pamela, and "storm in an artistic teacup" from Mr Brooke, she transferred all her attention to Philip Morgan.

"Any time now," he was saying. "We have to wait patiently because of Mr Carrington's expert doing it as a favour."

"No wonder David Lester's on edge."

"He's not the only one." Philip Morgan's hand just touched her shoulder, leaving a burning sensation that made her wish he would move away.

"I appreciate your trust over *Winter*." At least she could be professionally pleased about *that*. "All right, Philip." Anita gave her throaty chuckle. "Dinner it is." Phyllida had known from the moment of meeting him that she would eventually have to call on the fictions, and a dinner table would be as safe a place as any.

"When?"

"The day after tomorrow?" Friday night, which would mean she didn't have to see him the following morning, when the gallery would be closed.

"All right, Anita. Friday night. Your hotel?"

"I don't think so." A would-be lover hoping to join her in the minimal transition between the restaurant at the Golden Lion and her spartan office and changing room was so outrageously ludicrous a concept it had her more amused than dismayed. "Be more imaginative."

"I was being very imaginative indeed."

69

"Then that's too bad. I'd really prefer to eat somewhere else."

"Then you shall. I'll be thinking about it. Wherever I decide to take you, may I at least pick you up at the Golden Lion?"

"Of course."

"Seven-thirty?"

"Seven-thirty." Mrs Sunbury got to her feet and crossed to the table to deposit her teacup, aware of Mr Brooke's eyes on her. She had also been aware as she fenced with Philip Morgan of Pamela Bennett flouncing out and Thelma Royle flopping with a sigh into what was probably her favourite armchair. Thelma gave Anita a smile as she strolled to the door, and Anita forced Mr Brooke's quizzical look to turn into one in response to hers.

"Settling in, Mrs Sunbury?" he asked her.

"How could I fail to, Mr Brooke, with all these kind people?" As she strolled on, he made her the tribute of a bow.

Relieving Deborah at the Reception desk, Phyllida realised how much she was missing her team at Peter Piper, and when half-past five came Anita gratefully left the end of the day ritual to Deborah on the plea of an appointment and quickened her usual pace to Dawlish Square. Phyllida's instinct was to go straight up to the Agency, but thinking of Steve's reaction to Mrs Sunbury she went first to the Golden Lion, breaking into a run as she reached the narrow corridor with the thinner carpet.

It wasn't a thorough transformation, but it was enough to keep Steve's excitement professional. The latch was down on the Agency door and he and Jenny were playing a game of poker they both forgot the moment they saw Phyllida.

"We just hoped. . . ." Jenny said.

"We were just leaving," Steve told her.

Phyllida decided they had summed themselves up, and that she loved them both dearly. Along with Peter, who came blinking out of his office looking as if he had just come round from a doze.

"The wanderer returns," he greeted her. "Bring coffee through, you two? Unless Phyllida needs something sterner?"

"Coffee, please." She followed Peter into his room and took her usual chair in front of his desk.

"I know you'll want to share it," he said. "But is there anything better confined to my ears alone?"

"Not so far as today's concerned, I don't think." Philip Morgan's reaction to Anita Sunbury was part of the job and had to be common office knowledge, along with the physical necessity of Anita's lack of response. But Phyllida Moon's reaction to Philip Morgan wouldn't be shared with anyone. "Today I can regale you all. I've been awfully lucky."

"I expect that's a matter of opinion," Peter said, and repeated her words with a laugh when she had finished telling the three of them about her day. "The Lord helps those who help themselves."

"So much frustration, though!" Phyllida mourned.

"Think I should come in on it now, Gov?" Steve asked Peter. At the time he had chatted his employer up across the counter of the building society where he was languishing on the clerical staff, and secured himself the post of Peter's assistant in the field, he had been addicted to re-runs of *The Sweeney*. "It's stalemate on the warehouse job but I'm still hyped up to sitting around in the dark. I could get a takeaway and park in Marlborough Drive till midnight or so. Then go back in the morning. Say seven-thirty?" Phyllida nodded. "And follow the subject when he leaves. What d'you say, Gov?"

71

"I say it's fine if there's cover. If there isn't you could do more harm than good. Phyllida?"

"Facing out of the lane I think you could see anything or anyone approaching or leaving The Cedars. But you might make the people in the houses opposite uneasy. And I don't think there's any way a car parked till late at the kerb would escape observation."

"So unless you can call on Melanie," Peter said.

"Consider her called on," Steve said confidently. After seeing the adoring way his pale, skinny girlfriend had looked at him at the Christmas party, and the way he had scarcely looked at her at all, Phyllida had ceased to be surprised at Melanie's invariable agreement to help Steve give his surveillances the appearance of lovers' trysts – it could be the only way she got to spend any time alone with him.

"Disgusted residents of Marlborough Drive might still suggest you move on," Phyllida warned him. "But you won't have done any damage. You should be all right on your own in the lane in the morning."

"Killing time before an appointment, if anyone approaches you," Peter suggested.

"I'll ring Melanie and be off, then." Steve ambled to the door.

"Take care of her!" Peter ordered.

"Two takeaways!" Jenny decreed.

"Okay, okay. If I see anyone going into the house can I get out of the car and scout around?"

"Too risky," Phyllida said, looking at Peter.

Peter nodded. "But you'll follow Lester at both ends of the night if he leaves the house."

"Will do. Maybe see you in the morning, Miss Moon." Steve turned in the doorway to survey her wistfully. "That Philip Morgan. He's a lucky devil."

"Not a lucky one, Steve," Phyllida corrected him.

Chapter Six

When Mrs Cookson was ready to leave the room at the Golden Lion the next morning, Phyllida rang Steve mobile to mobile.

"Where and how are you?" she asked.

"Opposite the subject's house and effing cold."

"But bearing up bravely." Steve's habitual mingling of professional jargon and demotic was one of the things about him Phyllida enjoyed. "Anything happened?"

"Not so far as David Lester's concerned." She heard the ostentatious yawn. "Wasn't his fault I didn't get much sleep." So he'd gone home with Melanie at the end of his first vigil, and wanted Anita Sunbury to know.

"Your conscientiousness had its reward, then," Phyllida conceded. "I gather you're on your own now?"

"Yep. Got back here just before seven-thirty and there's been nothing happening. Any more than there was last night. A light was showing in the long window over the front door when we arrived at seven and it went out just after midnight, quarter of an hour after a dimmer one behind a downstairs curtain. That's when we packed it in." Steve gave a yelp of laughter, agreeably surprised by his crude pun.

Phyllida ignored it. "Landing and study." If David Lester had been spending the evening in his study it was unlikely he had had a visitor. "With the net curtains in the front you won't be able to see if the main curtain's been drawn back this morning."

"Right."

"Any trouble with parking?"

"Nope."

"That's a relief. I've been expecting a resident through a garden gate or at least a polite notice."

"The walls round the parking space and down the lane are pretty high and the trees are decorated with barbed wire. They must've decided that's enough, unless someone's having a party. You on your way?"

"This moment. If David Lester doesn't leave the house while I'm en route I suggest—"

"I'll back up into the parking space when I see you turn into Marlborough Drive, then resume my position and stay here, neighbours willing, until the subject emerges and I get on his tail."

"Fine," Phyllida approved humbly, suppressing a further suggestion that they ignore one another.

Mrs Cookson left the hotel as usual by the back door and got quickly into the car Phyllida had so far managed to park in a spot combining obscurity with unimpeded access to the car park exit. As she turned into the lane off Marlborough Drive Steve was reversing into the parking circle, and moved forward immediately she had entered it. Loping back down the lane, she saw his pale face through his driving mirror staring at her in red-eyed horror, but when she passed his open window he murmured, "Cheers", without looking up from the magazine propped against the steering wheel.

The moment she stepped on to pavement Phyllida was protected by the unlikelihood of anyone associating her car with Mrs Cookson, and at once slowed to the charlady's brisk but short-stepped gait, agreeably braced by her amusement at Steve's reaction to her appearance. She was so sure of David Lester still being at home that she rang the bell three times before using her key.

"Mr Lester? Hello-o-o. . . . It's only Mrs Cookson!"

74

The call was no more than her thespian expression of Mrs Cookson's old-fashioned awareness of her place: as she stepped into the dark hall Phyllida knew from the feel of the house that it was empty.

So David Lester had spent the night elsewhere. Or gone out in the small hours after turning off the landing light. . . .

Phyllida's shiver was involuntary; there were such things as time switches. Mrs Cookson bustled into the cloakroom and substituted her overall for her coat. Paper cracked under her stout shoes as she emerged, and in the gloom she had to grope about the autumn-tinted swirls of the hall carpet to find another manilla envelope. Phyllida's fingers probed the tucked-in flap as she moved over to the window and her disappointment was confirmed by the neat print of Mrs Everett's name and address which she read when she had opened the curtains. Pushing the envelope roughly into one of her large overall pockets she turned back to the hall.

It was a bright morning, and the gaping drawer of the hall table above the scatter of papers on the carpet was balefully clear even before her reluctant brain had made sense of it. The door of David Lester's study was ajar, and Phyllida ran across to it, hearing her panting breath as her fingers scrabbled for a light switch.

When she found and pressed it, a centre fitting illuminated a chaos which would have sent her sprawling if she had attempted to run straight to the window. Every drawer had been pulled out, every cupboard was open, and most of their contents, together with several of the drawers themselves, were tumbled about the floor. One of the two doors of the tall bookcase had been wrenched off its hinges, and books had been pulled out of every shelf and lay splayed among the scattered files and papers.

It was a scene of shocking disorder, but it heartened Phyllida because it lacked the one ingredient she had been dreading to see, despite trying to ridicule herself for being melodramatic: the body of David Lester slumped across his desk, despatched by his own hand as the climax of his brainstorm.

But when she took a second and slower look around the room, Phyllida saw that the two drawers which had been locked on her first circuit of the house had been forced open.

She picked her way back to the door and turned off the light, beginning to dread her thoughts. There had been no suicide because there had been no brainstorm. Someone other than David Lester had done violence to his belongings.

Could still be in his house.

Phyllida went quietly into the hall and stood listening.

To the same quality of silence that continued to advise her, despite her noisy heart and the evidence of destructive human energy all around her, that she was alone.

And whoever had entered the house would hardly have remained there beyond daybreak. There had been more than seven hours between Steve's two vigils, so it was hardly surprising he had seen no one, including David Lester himself. Whose overnight absence had obviously been known in advance by the intruder. . . .

Relieved to have recovered her commonsense, and reminding herself again about time switches, Phyllida went across to the drawing-room.

She would take a quick look around the whole house, and then she would call the Agency on the mobile phone she kept at the bottom of Mrs Cookson's large handbag.

The drawing-room had been as comprehensively attacked as the study had. The drawers of Mrs Everett's elegant Queen Anne chest had been wrenched out, and when

Phyllida lifted the dropped lid of the companion desk a splinter of walnut ran into her finger from beside the smashed lock. And in the small sanctum where Mrs Everett had interviewed Mrs Cookson the glass panels of the Regency chiffonier lay splintered on the carpet.

The kitchen door was stout and closed on a spring, and when Phyllida pushed it open the cold was so sudden and so sharp all she could focus on at first was the source of it: the hole in the window above the sink. Then she saw the long dresser drawer wedged at an angle with half its contents on the floor, and the bare table.

Shivering, she crossed the room. The broken glass had fallen into an empty sink, and had been crushed to crystals by the intruder's shoes on a clear draining-board – she could be certain David Lester hadn't breakfasted at home, and infer that he hadn't dined there either. Phyllida put her hand out to the back door, then thought better of it. And she knew without looking that the intruder would have had no trouble scaling the side gate whch had prevented Mrs Cookson from going round the back – it was made of patterned wrought iron, offering easy footholds.

Holding herself clear of the sink she looked through the cold gap and saw a robin perched on a support post in the kitchen garden. Waiting for Mr Daniels to come and turn up some worms. At the thought of Mr Daniels, Phyllida felt better again. And then she looked in the waste bin to confirm that it was as empty as she had left it the day before, and found the package that had contained the made-up fish dish David Lester had told her he was having for his dinner.

So he *had* had a meal before going out.

Going out . . . Phyllida went back to the hall, the enveloping warmth doing nothing for the growing chill of her spirits. Steve and Melanie had been in position at seven, and between then and their departure at midnight no one had left the house. And Anita Sunbury had been told by more than one employee of the Snaith Gallery that David Lester seldom went home before five-thirty. . . .

With her heart more acrobatic than she had known it on even the most potentially traumatic first night, Phyllida went slowly over to the stairs. There she paused, to fight the craven thought that it could be considered foolhardy to go upstairs alone, particularly with Steve so close at hand.

But it was what she believed Steve, and Peter, would do that had her moving again, and steadily climbing.

She went straight to David Lester's bedroom, pressing the light switch by the door as soon as she saw that the room was in darkness, so as to know the worst as quickly as possible.

But even under the bright overhead beam it took her a few ghastly seconds to make out that David Lester was lying neatly on his back in bed, because his solemn face was as pale as the white pillow and his pyjama jacket as red as the top sheet. The killer had gone for the throat, and the double bonus of a death both instant and silent. Lester hadn't even had time to start bringing his hands up from under the bed-clothes to defend himself. His eyes were open, but he had died too quickly to register so much as surprise and they stared expressionlessly at the ceiling. Apart from a spattering on the outer edges of the bedclothes the blood was concentrated close to the death wound – the throat had been cut into rather than sawn, and the murderer could have escaped without bloodstains.

Phyllida ran into the bathroom, and was just able to register that the lavatory bowl was empty before being sick into it. She put on her gloves before pulling the chain, then peered carefully about bathroom and bedroom, touching nothing but the lid of the linen basket and its contents – all that had been added to them since the previous morning was some underwear, no doubt dropped in by David Lester at his final bed-time.

Bracing herself, Phyllida went back into the bedroom and stood at the foot of the bed. Was there any possibility, she pleaded with herself, that David Lester could have cut his own throat?

Forcing her gaze on to the smooth turn-down of the sheet, the flat level shoulders indicating arms lying straight along the sides of the body, she knew, as she had known from the start, that there was not – even if the knife was found in or close to the bed. Someone had come into his bedroom while he slept and had committed murder.

Phyllida went thankfully out of the room and closed the door behind her. After looking into Mrs Everett's room and the guest bedroom, and finding them both ransacked, she sank to her knees on the landing and rang the Agency. It wasn't yet nine o'clock but it was worth a try.

Peter answered at once.

"Phyllida here. Steve's outside The Cedars and I'm inside. The house has been turned over and David Lester's dead in bed with his throat cut. I can't see a knife but it has to be murder, he's lying flat on his back with his arms under the bedclothes. Mrs Cookson will dial 9–9–9, but I thought I'd try you first. I'm not as calm as I sound, Peter."

"I don't suppose you are. But you're all right?"

"Yes."

"Good. Any signs of a break in?"

"Through the kitchen window. Will you ring Steve and tell him there's no point in hanging on? And Peter . . . when the police question Mrs Cookson she won't be able to tell them she's staying at the Golden Lion."

"She'll tell them she's a private detective engaged by Lester's sister through the Peter Piper Agency because of her worries about his reaction to an anonymous letter. The police owe us, remember, for having solved their Claire College murders for them."

"So I'll have to break Mrs Everett's confidence."

"Her brother's been murdered, Phyllida."

"Yes. I'm glad you let me join your staff under a phoney name."

"Your anonymity in all directions being of the essence. You've got your ID with you?"

"Of course. The police will ask for an address too, Peter."

"And it's care of The Peter Piper Detective Agency. They had to accept that last time. Look, don't go back into Lester's bedroom."

"I won't. Thanks. I'm all right now. D'you want me to come clean at the Gallery as well?"

"Oh, Lord, let me have a quick think. They'll want potted biographies of all the staff. . . . You *can* say Anita Sunbury's staying at the Golden Lion, of course, but I think you should tell the truth about her as well. With your skills they're bound to discover sooner or later that Mary Bowden's an overall name for my whole team of female field workers, the way Hoover's an overall name for vacuum cleaners, so they might as well decide sooner. And adding the revelation about Anita to the revelation about Mrs Cookson is only showing the extent of the Agency's efficiency and initiative."

"Point taken. And telling them about Mrs Cookson should at least ensure I get to the Gallery by the time I'm expected to be there. . . . Peter, shall I make the two revelations together?"

"Why not? It'll give the police time to take in the implications of Anita's position before they meet her. And I'll back you up, I'll ring the police myself. I've already got something to offer them with Steve's vigils. I'll wait till I've given them time to believe you put your

80

citizen's duty first and gave priority to dialling 9–9–9. You'd better do that now."

"I will. Thanks, Peter."

"Thank *you*. I'm sorry, Phyllida. I wish it had been me." Peter tried to keep the envy he was feeling out of his voice. Three years in the business hadn't brought him a corpse, and here was his assistant being granted one within months of entering it.

"You'll be in the office tonight?"

"Of course."

Phyllida buried her phone at the bottom of Mrs Cookson's bag and hurried downstairs, moving back into her character as she ran. She had been so reassured by her talk with Peter the hardest part of her distress call was restoring her sense of acute agitation.

"Fire, police or ambulance?"

"Oh . . ." Pause for some noticeably gasping breaths. "Police! It's police I want! There's been a murder!"

"All right, madam, if you'll just try and stay calm I'll put you through."

Mrs Cookson's agitation had not infected the woman to whom she had conveyed it. Phyllida wondered how many such frantic statements turned out to be true. The police contact was equally phlegmatic. When she had given him Mrs Cookson's name and the address of The Cedars he told her to wait quietly somewhere out of sight of the occurrence.

His choice of word had Phyllida rather than Mrs Cookson giggling wildly as she hung up, a warning that she must allow for the fact that she was still in shock. As she regained control of herself, she realised that the arrival of Mr Daniels was no longer something to look forward to. She would not let Mrs Cookson react as she should to the sight of him and go flying down the path screaming her news, but even so, he might see the broken glass for himself, which would draw him into the house and eventually up the stairs to David Lester's bedroom, leaving a set of foot and finger prints to distract the police.

At least it was his habit to enter the garden through the garage on the other side of the house where he kept his tools, and the broken window didn't directly face the garden. There was still an hour to go before he would expect his summons to coffee, so with luck he might remain unalerted until the arrival of the police. Phyllida went back into the kitchen and cautiously approached the window. Mr Daniels was working, obligingly, at the very bottom of his vegetable patch, and as she moved away she saw the robin fly towards him and settle on a cabbage stalk to watch him at work with his spade.

Mrs Cookson could well be too distressed by her discovery to get farther than the hall, and Phyllida went back there and sat down on the edge of one of the severe chairs, acting the distressed charlady for all she was worth. She must remain convincingly in character until she had decided when, and to which member or members of the police team she would confess her charade. Panic returned as she saw her own vulnerable self about to be revealed, but receded as she realised she would in fact be disclosing another false identity which would present no outward appearance, protected as it would be by the Mrs Cookson exterior, and then by Anita Sunbury. Mary Bowden – who had a slight Scottish accent – would be a Hoover figure from the moment of her birth. . . .

This time Phyllida's amusement was under her control, as was the hysterical woman who, ten minutes later, let the police into the house.

"Upstairs!" Mrs Cookson gasped. "In 'is own bed! First left at the top o' the stairs. I ain't touched nothing. And the 'ole 'ouse turned over. . . ." Mrs Cookson sank down on the hall carpet, whence both uniformed policemen gently lifted her and placed her on a chair.

One of them knelt beside her and held her shoulders between strong hands while the other pushed each downstairs door open in turn and peered inside.

"Kitchen window's broke," Mrs Cookson moaned.

The journeying policeman came out of the kitchen nodding his head. "She's right. That's how he got in. Best stay where you are, love, there's nowhere else for you to sit without maybe messing up the evidence. Now, you all right while we take a look round upstairs?"

"You better take a deep breath," Mrs Cookson advised, casting her anguished gaze from one policeman to the other. "I'm telling you . . . I've never been so shocked in all me life, and Mr Lester such a nice, kind man."

The kneeling policeman released her shoulders with a squeeze and got to his feet, one of his bones going off like a pistol shot as he straightened up. Phyllida saw both men pause at the foot of the stairs and consciously square their shoulders. "Stay where you are now, love," the senior one said to her as they started up.

Within seconds she heard both God and His Son hoarsely invoked, and then there was silence broken by the odd murmur and movement of feet before the sharp crackle introducing the jerky narrative of the phone-in. Mrs Cookson would wait with the two horrified uniforms for the team they were summoning, and reveal herself as Mary Bowden to the CID. Meanwhile she'd rally, and the uniforms would recall with admiration what they'd been told about the working class spirit during the war and be heartened to discover that it was still there to be called on in an emergency. . . . A reshowing of the picture of David Lester lying murdered in his bed pulled Phyllida clear of her actress's ego. A picture she was afraid she would always be able to conjure up, even if eventually it ceased to take her by surprise.

The policemen were clattering back down the stairs.

"We're sorry you found him, love. The scene of crimes

officer and the doctor are on their way, and then the CID'll be here and you can make your statement and be off home. We'd like to have made you a nice cup of tea while we're waiting, but the intruder came in by the kitchen window, didn't he, and we can't risk disturbing any evidence."

"That's all right, I'll survive. You going to tell Mr Daniels, then? 'E'll be expecting 'is coffee."

The uniformed posteriors rose hastily from the chairs they had been about to contact. "If you'll be so good, constable," the senior man suggested.

"If you say so, sarge." The constable shrugged his shoulders and slowly crossed the hall. As the stout door wheezed inward there was instant chill.

"I ain't touched the back door, neither," Mrs Cookson called after him. "But I spex it's unlocked. You can see the bolts is drawn. And 'e wouldn't of climbed *out* of the window, would 'e?"

"No," said the constable, disappearing on another admiring glance.

"You're being very brave, Mrs Cookson," the sergeant said. Phyllida suspected he felt suddenly at a loss. "But you've had a terrible shock."

"That's a fact," Mrs Cookson agreed. "And I still can't believe it."

"The CID will take your official statement, but while we're waiting and while things are vivid . . . Perhaps you'd like to tell me just informally about your arrival this morning. You got here in the usual way?"

"That's right," Phyllida responded truthfully, realizing how much easier it was going to be to come clean, and hoping she would not be asked in the meantime, with Mr Daniels at hand, to tell the truth. "And when I'd rung the bell three times I used my key. Mr Lester give me one in case 'e left early. I called out, o' course, but I 'ad the feeling the second I was in the 'all that I 'ad the 'ouse to meself.' Mrs Cookson choked on a shocked sob, but visibly rallied. "When I seen the mess in the 'all I went all through downstairs and it was all the same. Then I went upstairs and found 'im. Mr Lester. Such a kind man. . . ." This time tears prevailed, and Phyllida saw the relief in the sergeant's eyes as the kitchen door opened to admit the constable and Mr Daniels.

Mr Daniels had his cap in his hand and was punishing his tonsure.

"You should of told me!" he gasped accusingly at Mrs Cookson. Phyllida saw that he was trembling from head to foot. "Mr Lester's my friend!"

"Me legs wouldn't take me no farther than the 'all," Mrs Cookson sobbed, "and that's the truth, Mr Daniels. I don't know as 'ow I managed to dial 9–9–9."

But Mr Daniels was continuing to glare at her with a mixture of reproach and suspicion, and might well tell the police how long Mrs Cookson had been working at The Cedars without their asking. It was a relief to hear the front door bell while he was still lamenting his loss.

The large and disparate crowd ascending the staircase suggested that the various essential groups had coincided in the drive. The uniformed men were instantly to attention, but the constable stood beside Mrs Cookson and volunteered information on the passing throng, which Phyllida, in the interests of her other career, wished she could have thanked him for.

But he didn't mention the CID. "The detectives, then?" Mrs Cookson asked casually.

"They come last, when the experts have done."

"And when'll that be?"

"Couple of hours at the most."

The local chief superintendent CID was there with a sergeant just after half past eleven.

Mrs Cookson was identified to them before they went upstairs, and when they came down after their

85

first, short, visit to the deathbed, the uniformed sergeant told them she was particularly anxious to talk to them.

"And we to talk to her," the super said affably.

"I suggest the guest bedroom, sir," the uniformed sergeant put forward diffidently. "It's been turned over like everywhere else and there could be evidence, of course, but it appears to be empty, apart from a slight overflow in wardrobe and drawers. First on the right, if Mrs Cookson feels up to going upstairs again."

"Bless you, I'm all right," Mrs Cookson reassured them.

Behind the closed door of the guest bedroom, alone with the two CID men, Phyllida rummaged in Mrs Cookson's bag and produced her ID card along with her soft Edinburgh accent.

"I'm Mary Bowden and I work for the Peter Piper Detective Agency. Mr Lester's sister engaged the Agency because she was worried—"

"We know about you, Miss Bowden, and we're grateful for the way you've handled your discovery of this unhappy occurrence." This time Phyllida didn't find the word so funny, and the superintendent looked exasperated rather than grateful. "We hope we can expect a full and frank statement from you of everything you may have discovered this week as well as what happened this morning."

"Yes, of course. The only thing is—"

"That Mary Bowden is expected at the Snaith Gallery at two o'clock this afternoon." The chief superintendent glanced with annoyance at his watch. "It is now twelve noon, and as your employer does not admit to the fact that Mary Bowden is a general name for his female operatives, I am constrained to keep up the fiction that she will need time to discard one disguise and assume another. I shall therefore expect her to present herself at my office in Lavender Street this evening directly she leaves the Gallery."

It was obvious he would not be satisfied by an assurance that Anita Sunbury could provide all the statement he needed. "Thank you, I appreciate that. But please – keeping up the fiction means Mary Bowden will need time again. May she present herself within an hour of her departure from the Gallery? That could be quite early," Phyllida added encouragingly. "In view of what's happened the director could decide to close for the day."

The chief superintendent sighed. "This is all rather trying but yes, I suppose so." Because he needed her. And that need was what had made him agree to accept Mary Bowden as the nearest he would get to identifying Peter Piper's female personnel.

"Thank you. I – Mary Bowden is working at the Snaith Gallery as a receptionist under the name of Anita Sunbury. Which I expect you know."

"I know," the chief superintendent responded wearily.

Under the surprised eyes of the uniformed men and Mr Daniels, the CID sergeant let Mrs Cookson out of the house a mere ten minutes after she had gone upstairs. Phyllida was shocked, in the light of her hideous discovery, to find herself having to suppress a smile.

Chapter Seven

Chief Superintendent Maurice Kendrick of Seaminster CID stopped just inside the door of the Snaith Gallery's staff rest room, his Sergeant Wetherhead beside him, and surveyed the assembled members of the Gallery's staff.

"Thank you all for joining me here," he said, when he had decided Mary Bowden had to be the plain scowling woman with the shiny nose and had mentally panned her for over-acting. "Let me begin by offering you my condolences for the tragic loss of your colleague." He might end up arresting one of them for murder, but he had to acknowledge that as a group they had suffered a bereavement. And he had been highly impressed by the violence of the old gardener's reaction to his employer's death. Given a genuine strength of feeling, anger and resentment could be effectively presented as loyalty and affection, and the old man had been unable to offer an alibi. . . .

"Thank you," the Gallery's director responded, as formally. Charles Carrington was standing to the side of his small team, but still conveyed the impression of leading it. It wasn't just his tall, well-dressed figure, Kendrick decided, it was also the air of serious yet kindly authority which almost visibly surrounded him. "We appreciate your attitude to our tragedy, Chief Superintendent." Kendrick would have taken a bet that Charles Carrington would get his rank right. "Is it in order for me to ask for any information you are in a position to give us about – about what happened? You'll appreciate how concerned we all are. And – not knowing anything can be even more distressing than knowing the worst."

"I appreciate your feelings, sir." But he was ready to disband the mutual admiration society. "And I can tell you the facts as they appear at the moment." Kendrick paused, reluctantly recalling his reaction to his visit to the victim's bedroom and trying to find words to ease the impact of what he had been invited to say. "Mr Lester was asleep in bed when he was attacked and obviously died instantly. His throat was cut." It was impossible to know the precise location of the sharply drawn breaths, who had moaned and who had whinnied, but there was shock and horror to be seen in all seven faces, even though the woman he was calling Mary Bowden looked resentful of having her emotions hijacked, a reaction he grudgingly allowed to be in keeping with the character she was so unsubtly trying to project. "The house appears to have been broken into via a window in the kitchen, and every room has been turned over." *Between the hours of 12.15 and 7.15 a.m.*, Kendrick added in his mind, feeling anything but grateful to the source of that information and then, to his relief, finding himself amused by this manifestation of an inflated *amour propre* and realising he had regained his sense of humour. "As you of course all know, David Lester lived with his sister. Who is away this week. Perhaps some of you know that, too."

The words were so provocative Kendrick uttered them with particular mildness, smiling reassuringly as he made his second survey of the room. There was no reaction from Mary Bowden, but she was a rotten actress and her judgment wasn't much better, starting at such a high pitch of irritability she had left herself nowhere to go. On the other faces there was slowly dawning comprehension, followed in the face of the small fat secretary by indignation. Two of them continued to seem

89

detached from what was going on: the tall, sophisticat-
edly attractive woman leaning gracefully against a chair
looked merely interested, and the youngish man who was
aware of both her and his own good looks appeared to be
enjoying himself.

The frailly lean older man with the near-skeletal face
said softly, "Yes, I did. Edward Brooke. David Lester told
me at the beginning of the week that he was on his own
at home. It was uncharacteristic because he was usually
reserved about himself, but I think he was annoyed that
his sister had decided to engage a daily woman to come
in during her absence. He said she often went away and
had always let the usual arrangement run – one of those
teams of cleaners who go all through a house once a
week. But this time, for the first time, she'd insisted
on appointing this daily. I've a good memory, and I
remember particularly well what David said because of
its being out of character. I don't know if that is of any
help, Chief Superintendent."

"Indeed it is, Mr Brooke. Thank you." If it hadn't
been for Peter Piper and his eponymous operative it
would have been very helpful indeed, and the interest
it aroused in him would have been born now instead of
a couple of hours ago when Piper had told him about Mrs
Everett's distressed request. And an anonymous letter,
which, by the time he got back to the office, should be
on his desk.

"So David Lester behaved uncharacteristically," Kendrick
said, this time surveying the gathering with a question in
his eyes and voice. "Did he behave uncharacteristically
in any other way in, say, the past few weeks?"

Several voices responded with instant affirmatives.
Kendrick was able to distinguish three: the amused man's
which was offhand, the secretary's which was emphatic,
and the director's, which was its usual measured self.

"Yes, sir?" Kendrick asked the director.

90

"David was – worried. I saw it myself, and other members of staff remarked on it to me. He was always an undemonstrative man, but at the same time he was friendly and approachable and showed an interest in other people and their concerns. For the past few weeks he's seemed to be – well, someone called it far away, and I think that describes his recent behaviour pretty well. But he was jumpy, too, as if he was afraid of something." Mr Carrington paused, took a deep breath, and squared his well-tailored shoulders.

"Yes, sir?"

"There's something I think I must say. Something I learned this morning and was intending to tell my staff before the end of the day. Chief Superintendent, may I have your word that it will not reach the media via you or your colleagues?"

"You have it," Kendrick readily replied.

"That's right," DS Wetherhead assured the Director, after a discreet nudge from his senior.

"Thank you. I ask the same of my staff." Charles Carrington paused, nodding his response to the assenting murmur. "You'll know of course, Chief Superintendent, Sergeant, about the anonymous arrival here of the two paintings by Frederick Sandys, and the excitement aroused nationally when they were authenticated. In each case we kept the arrivals secret until we knew that the pictures were genuine. My staff were totally co-operative both times, and I'm very grateful to them."

Kendrick caught a swift expressionless glance pass between the man and the women he was calling, in the essential initial shorthand of his police profession, the two comparatively glamorous members of the staff.

"This morning I had my expert's verdict on the third picture." As Mr Carrington gazed steadily at Kendrick, the Chief Superintendent realised his urbane face had become worn and ravaged without appearing to change its expression. "It's a fake."

This time the reaction was universal. Mary Bowden hammed her horror to the extent of banging her fist on the table beside her. He would have to ask Piper to tell her to take it easy or put someone else in her place.

"No!" she shouted.

The offhand young man said "My God!" with intense feeling.

"I'm afraid there's no doubt about it." The director managed a solacing smile round the gathering. "The picture itself is as convincing as the other two so far as the painting's concerned, but the materials are modern. This, of course, has to call the authenticity of the first two in question, although my personal faith in them holds up and I still believe Sandys carried out his intention of working up his *Spring* sketch into a picture, and painted *Summer*." Mr Carrington paused. "There was a longer time gap between the arrival of *Summer* and *Winter* than between *Spring* and *Summer*, and I now suspect that when a genuine *Winter* failed to materialise someone was unable to resist supplying his or her own version. But that isn't the concern at the moment of the Chief Superintendent, and we must hope it never will be."

"I hope not, too," Kendrick said, finding himself pitying the man and at the same time admiring him for the unflinching stoicism which was enabling him to retain his considerable dignity. "And I'm aware that you've shared your bad news with me and my colleague only because you feel it may have some bearing on David Lester's state of mind. And perhaps on his death."

"Yes. He is – was – our expert on the Pre-Raphaelite Brotherhood, which had so strong an influence on Frederick Sandys. When the first picture arrived – *Spring* – he was intensely excited, and appeared convinced from the start that it was genuine. Likewise with *Summer*." Mr

92

Carrington paused again. "And apparently with *Winter*."
He turned slightly, to put his weight against a chair.
"Chief Superintendent, this is a very difficult thing
for me to say. If there is any connection between the
revelation of this forgery and David Lester's death, then
one feels totally bewildered that he should have been
murdered. Whereas one can just envisage that if he had
been involved in the fraud he could have taken his own
life, through shame or fear. Is there no possibility that
he did?"

"None at all, I'm afraid," Kendrick said steadily.

"I see. Then we must hope he had nothing to do
with the fraud. That his murder is a ghastly coincidence.
Unless. . . ."

"Yes, sir?"

"I'm sorry, Chief Superintendent, I was thinking aloud.
Pure speculation. When I give you my statement. . . ."

"Of course, sir." Kendrick again smiled round the
group. "We must all hope Mr Lester's office files will
yield some information, of whatever kind." The house
had been turned over so thoroughly he wasn't hopeful of
there being much, if any, information awaiting discovery
there, but he had been slightly encouraged to find that
one of the drawers in the murder victim's office filing
cabinet was locked and that there appeared to be no
second key to it in the gallery. If the burglar/murderer
had taken one from the house he hadn't been able to
make use of it.

Unless he or she was a member of staff. . . .

And even then. . . . On his way through the Gallery,
Kendrick had noted the minuteness of the staff offices,
and that all the doors stood wide open. And the Director
had told him, in the few moments he had enjoyed the
hospitality of the only fair-sized private office, that
although all but the most junior and temporary members
of staff had keys to the outer door, they could not be

used when the burglar alarm was in operation without alerting the police.

So if there had ever been anything in that locked drawer which could throw light on David Lester's murder, Kendrick reckoned on it still being there.

"My men should soon complete the clearing of Mr Lester's office," he told them. "And the forensic experts will have done all they need to do there by the end of the afternoon. I appreciate your willingness to close the Gallery to the public, Mr Carrington."

"It was our wish as well as yours, Chief Superintendent." The Director had negotiated his painful hurdle as smoothly as possible, and regained his urbanity. "There's no way we could have conducted any business today."

Kendrick noted another subdued murmur of agreement. "Of course. I understand. Now, I should like to talk to each of you individually so that Sergeant Wetherhead can take down your statements. And I'll be grateful if you can hang on in the Gallery until I've seen you all, in case I have anything else then to say to you collectively. Mr Carrington? I don't suggest turning this room into my interview room as there will obviously be a need for teas and coffees. Can you fix us up somewhere?"

"Of course. Not ideal, but I hope you'll find it adequate. If you'd like to come with me, Chief Superintendent."

Kendrick heard the immediate subdued babble springing up behind them as the door closed. The Director led the way to another door in the wall as unapparent as his own. This time no daylight met them, and he clicked a switch.

"Our ground floor storeroom. Without a window, I'm afraid, but the lack of one takes a good chunk off our insurance premium and offers some peace of mind."

"I'm sure it does." Kendrick wondered idly what a plan of the rambling old building would look like.

The square space was lit by a powerful overhead light and the only furniture was a mahogany table and four balloon-backed chairs. There was no wall decoration, as all the wall space, from floor to ceiling, was taken up with graduated fitments enabling pictures to be slotted in sideways, the largest at the foot. Without the fitments, Kendrick saw as he looked round, they would have been standing in a very large room.

"This will be fine," he said. And the harsh lighting and sense of being cut off from the outside world, which made the space feel like a high-class interrogation cell, could concentrate a few minds. "Now, perhaps you would like to be our first interviewee, Mr Carrington?" Kendrick had been trying unsuccessfully since his arrival to decide why the Director of the Snaith Gallery seemed vaguely familiar, and suddenly found the context: Carrington had been pointed out to him at a civic junketing a month or so back as an influential member of the local Arts establishment. The memory brought a rush of increased respect for him. The disauthentication of his precious *Winter* would be a devastating blow to a man who had established a reputation for artistic knowledge and probity, and if the forgery became publicly known, as would surely happen eventually, it could affect the standing of his Gallery in view of its sale of two other paintings under the name of Frederick Sandys. To say nothing of Carrington's personal reaction to the violent death of a senior member of his staff.

"Was David Lester a personal friend of yours?" Kendrick asked, as Carrington sat down to face him and Sergeant Wetherhead across the expanse of gleaming mahogany – another plus to the Gallery and its direction, as if the table had been expressly polished in readiness for police use of it.

"We got on very well," the Director said slowly, "without being personal friends. I mean, Chief Superintendent,

95

that David was a valued and trusted member of my staff, but we scarcely met away from the gallery. When I've had a big party I've invited him and his sister, and I've been to a party at his house, but that's as far as it went. As far as it goes with any members of my staff, for that matter, and I think I can say I get on well with them all."

"Thank you, sir, that's very helpful. So if Mr Lester had had any worries he would have been unlikely to bring them to you?"

"If they were personal worries, I should say highly unlikely. I'd have expected him to bring any worries connected with his work. Which means that if it *does* appear that he was – involved in the presentation of *Winter* as a picture by Frederick Sandys . . . and that he perpetrated a fraud with *Spring* and *Summer* as well. . . ." Charles Carrington closed his eyes for a moment in which his face again aged – "I shall find it very hard to believe. *Spring* reached us six months ago, and David appeared to be quite wild with excitement. As he was over *Summer*, which arrived a couple of months later. To have put on a false reaction, and maintained it over several months . . . well, I can't imagine anyone capable of that, let alone David Lester. So I have to believe, at least unless and until it's proved otherwise, that if he is involved it's only with *Winter*, and that *Spring* and *Summer* are genuine Sandys. I'm saying that because of my regard for David, Chief Inspector, as well as out of my own conviction about the two earlier pictures and my concern for my Gallery."

"I appreciate that, sir." Kendrick did. "I think you were about to say something when I was talking to you all just now?"

"Ah." Carrington exhaled a long breath. "I was about to introduce the character of the man – or woman – who painted *Winter*. One thing we know for certain is that it couldn't have been David himself."

"You're sure of that?"

"Oh, yes. David wasn't any sort of an artist. We – art experts – very rarely are, Mr Kendrick. What I was wondering – am wondering – is whether he and the person who devised the scam fell out. Whether the painter was blackmailing the man who had commissioned him. If that man was David. . . ."

"Wouldn't you expect the victim to be the one to lash out?" DS Wetherhead asked.

"I don't think we can expect anything at the moment," Kendrick said firmly, uneasy to find himself discussing the possibilities in a murder case with someone who was technically a suspect. And he hadn't had time or space since the Director's revelation to bring a putative forger into his mental field of suspects. "Certainly not before we've spoken to Mrs Everett and discovered if any valuables are missing." Part of the killer's intention could have been theft. Only part: there was no way he – or she – could have killed in self defence; the murder of David Lester had been planned. "But thank you for sharing your thoughts with us, Mr Carrington. Now, can you tell me anything about David Lester's relations with other members of your staff?"

"I don't think he had any, Chief Superintendent. I think he was just on general good terms with them the way he was with me. I think you'll find the staff as well as myself telling you the only time they got a look at David Lester's personal reactions was when he was so excited about the Sandys. Don't misunderstand me, I'm not trying to say he was reclusive or unsociable, it was just that he was I think reticent by nature, and also that any social life he led had no connection with his working life."

"He never brought a partner to any Gallery function?"

"He brought his sister a couple of times." Charles Carrington hesitated, leaned forward. "Chief Inspector. . . ."

"Yes?"

"I did gather . . . I was in a group with David and his sister at one of those functions, and a young woman – not, I'm happy to say, a member of my staff – who had had a glass of wine too many said cheekily that she'd like to see Mr Lester 'partying' – I remember that odious verb, it suited her – with a girlfriend rather than a sister. I suppose she could have been proposing herself for the position in a roundabout way, but the atmosphere was very light-hearted and I was surprised by the strength of David's reaction – he told the girl to mind her own business and left everyone embarrassed. That was probably why Mrs Everett came up to me later and told me David's break-up with his wife had been very bitter and had left him wary of forming another attachment. I'm sorry, Chief Superintendent." Charles Carrington leaned back in his chair. "This is probably quite irrelevant to your inquiry, but it's all I can offer."

"And I'm grateful for it. You're married, Mr Carrington?"

"I am."

"I don't suppose. . . . Did your wife ever make any comment on David Lester? Was she present at the incident you've just told me about? A woman's intuition. . . ." Kendrick ended vaguely, trying to feel as detached as he hoped he was managing to sound. His own marriage had ended in bitterness and he, too, was wary of forming another attachment. For a moment his attention turned inward, and when he had it back under control Carrington had begun his reply.

". . . don't think she was with me at that point. I may or may not have mentioned the incident to her, I don't remember, but she hardly saw enough of David to offer any comment on him. Even over the Sandys I would say she was too interested in what they meant to the gallery and to me to be interested in David's reactions."

"Yes, of course." Kendrick shifted in his chair, reluctant to offer another assault on Carrington's gallantly maintained dignity. "I'm sorry about my next question, sir, but I think you'll appreciate that I have to ask it of everyone who knew David Lester as a matter of routine. Can you tell me where you were last night between midnight and seven a.m.?"

"I can, Chief Superintendent." Kendrick was relieved that the man hadn't flinched. "I was at home. I'd driven from London and didn't get back until – oh, it must have been about eleven. My wife will probably be able to tell you. She was ready for bed but was waiting for me downstairs and we had a drink before going up together. My alarm went off as usual at a quarter past seven."

"Thank you, Mr Carrington." Kendrick turned to DS Wetherhead, and there was silence for a moment as the sergeant finished writing. "That is really all we need from you by way of a statement. If you'd just like to read it and then sign it if you agree it's a fair account of some of the things you've told us." He was getting impatient and Carrington seemed to take a long time, although when he reached the end of the short document he signed it without comment. "Thank you. And now. . . ."

"Mr Kendrick. . . ."

"Yes?"

"I know this isn't the right question at such a time, but . . . David Lester and his sister have some wonderful furniture. Did the – the intruder – damage anything?"

"I saw a couple of smashed bureau locks in the drawing-room and what seems to be Mrs Everett's small sitting-room. Beyond that I don't know."

"A-a-h." Charles Carrington shuddered and closed his eyes again, then smiled as he opened them. It was a nice smile, with a rueful edge. "I'm sorry."

"That's all right, sir. Now, could I ask you to send in . . ." Kendrick pretended to look at the list of names in front of him. "Anita Sunbury? It doesn't matter in what order I see your staff, but we have to begin somewhere. Is Miss Sunbury a senior member?"

"No, she's a temporary receptionist, she's only been with us this week. So perhaps you'd rather—"

"She won't take up much of our time, then, so we might as well get her out of the way. If you'll be so good, sir?"

"Yes, of course, Chief Superintendent."

The Director got to his feet and walked over to the door. "Thank you very much, Mr Carrington," Kendrick said as he reached it, penitent and hoping his impatience hadn't shown. "I'm extremely grateful for your co-operation."

"What else?"

The rueful smile again, and Kendrick thought vaguely it was a pity that at the moment it couldn't appear more often. But within seconds his thoughts were off the gallery director. "You'll have to concoct some form of statement," he told the sergeant. "Using what she says where you can. Did you pick her out? Mary Bowden?" He was amused by his excitement and slightly ashamed of his eagerness to deflate Peter Piper's clever dick. He would have to rein it in.

"I wouldn't like to say," Wetherhead responded warily.

"Your caution does you credit I suppose, Jim."

"You'd stick your neck out then, sir?"

"If you have to put it that way, yes. I'd say it was obvious."

So he was annoyed and frustrated when the woman who joined them in the storeroom was the tall, glamorous American. She strolled up to the table.

"I asked to see Anita Sunbury," he accused her, as mildly as he could manage.

"That's why I'm here, Chief Superintendent. Mary Bowden, alias Anita Sunbury." At The Cedars, Phyllida

100

had felt constrained to abandon Mrs Cookson's voice, but decided she could be as convincing a detective in Anita Sunbury's as in Mary Bowden's. To his further annoyance, Kendrick found the husky American tones as attractive as the looks. He ignored Sergeant Wetherhead's sudden paroxysm of coughing. "Please sit down, Mrs. . . ."

"I would appreciate Mrs Sunbury on these premises."

"Yes, of course." It was an absurd pretence, that this elegant woman and the old-fashioned charwoman he had seen that morning were one and the same person. But Piper had come up with the goods once and showed signs of doing it again, so that humouring him should be easy enough.

Only it wasn't. Kendrick was still just managing to be amused by the situation but he didn't like it, nor the feeling his reactions were giving him – that he was more blokish than he had suspected.

"Now, Mrs Sunbury. Will you be good enough to tell me anything you've learned since you joined the Gallery staff?"

Mrs Sunbury settled into the balloon-backed chair as if it were the most comfortable place she had ever sat. "After just three afternoons I'm afraid there isn't much. But I can bear out what Mr Carrington said about David Lester's behaviour, and Mrs Cookson will tell you the same thing when you see her later today." The Chief Superintendent showed no signs of accepting Mesdames Cookson and Sunbury as one and the same, so she had to go along with him. "Even without knowing him as he apparently used to be, I could see he was desperately nervous and worried – when I passed his open door once he was banging his head against his filing cabinet. But. . . ."

"Yes?" prompted the sergeant.

"Since I heard the news of the murder I've kept telling myself he must have known he was in mortal danger, but

101

he gave – both me and Mrs Cookson – the impression of being worried rather than frightened. As if he was afraid for his reputation rather than his life." And maybe for the reputation of someone else. She had had an instinct to protect "the profile" from the moment of seeing it, and Peter had agreed to her plea that for the time being they keep its presence at The Cedars to themselves.

"That would fit with the threat in the anonymous letters and the latest picture being a fake," the sergeant observed.

"Yes," Kendrick said shortly. He had no more wish for a police discussion of the case in the presence of a private detective than in the presence of a technical suspect. But it could be that the sender of the letters and the murderer were two unconnected people. "Have you learned anything about any other member of staff which you feel might have a bearing on David Lester's death and/or the anonymous letters?"

"Not much." Phyllida passed on her impressions. "I'll hope to do better. Philip Morgan's laying siege to Mrs Sunbury, so that may yield something over dinner for two. I gather from my boss you're willing for me to stay on at the Gallery while you're investigating the murder?"

"Yes," Kendrick said, as abruptly. He knew it made sense, and tried again to subdue the resentment which had been baulked of the anticipated pleasure of criticising Peter Piper's agent. There was nothing he could fault in this woman, and nothing – to his ashamed relief – he had to thank her for, either. But he had the wits and experience to know that before another week was out he might be grateful for the multiple presence of Mary Bowden. "If you will," he added, as ungrudgingly as he could manage. "And of course make the most of Morgan's interest, it could be useful. I think that's all for now, thank you. If you'll just look over what the sergeant's written, and sign it if you're in agreement that it's a fair record of – certain of the things you've told us. No doubt you know I'm seeing Mrs Cookson later today," he added, when Mrs Sunbury had complied.

"Yes." Phyllida wasn't looking forward to the slog of so unnecessary a transformation, but she'd make the most of it and offer Mrs C's condolences to Mrs Everett after she'd seen the Chief Superintendent again. . . .

"Would you ask Miss Bennett to come in now, please?"

Miss Bennett was as trying as Kendrick had feared she would be. As Piper's agent had said, she appeared to be more interested in painting than in people and offered them a critique of the public's attitude to art before denying having noticed any change in David Lester's behaviour.

Edward Brooke gave an unsolicited character reference to Lester, behind which Kendrick thought he could detect sincerity, and the impression of knowing rather more than he was prepared to put into words about his extant colleagues. The Chief Superintendent felt he was expected to draw enlightening inferences from a few gnomic remarks, but failed to do so. Brooke took longer than both policemen thought necessary to read through and sign his short statement, which was also trying. But the old boy was obviously observant and intelligent, and Kendrick was afraid he might have to come back to him and attempt to call his bluff.

Director's secretary Thelma Royle seemed to be torn between an almost physical nausea at the idea of the throat-cutting and a frantic anxiety about the well-being of Mr Carrington and the Gallery, and offered no insights. Receptionist Deborah Handley said she wouldn't ever have believed an art gallery could be so exciting, and Philip Morgan said, with an expressionless face, that David Lester was the last person one would imagine getting involved in mayhem and murder, and that although he found the implications shattering he couldn't stop asking himself Shelley's question.

"Yes, sir?"

"Oh, you know. *If Winter comes, can Spring be far behind?*"

Chapter Eight

"Er . . . Miss Bowden?"

"Sir?" Mrs Cookson smiled obligingly at Detective Chief Superintendent Kendrick, and Phyllida felt sorry for the tall, curly-haired policeman who needed both her and his authority and was finding them difficult bedfellows.

"You – you'll be seeing Mrs Everett again?"

"I'm going to her when I leave here, she's asked to see Mrs Cookson," Phyllida told him and his sergeant truthfully. Peter had rung her on her mobile at the Golden Lion while she was changing, to tell her Mrs Everett had begged him to send Mrs Cookson to her. "Because I found him, I suppose. Not that I can tell her anything to help her."

The Chief Superintendent cleared his throat. "I didn't quite gather. . . . What is Mrs Everett's – perception of Mrs Cookson?"

"She sees her as a working-class woman with a sideline, a sort of private investigator's informant." Kendrick found the soft, educated Scottish voice an unsettling contrast to Mrs Cookson's unrefined appearance. "When she first went there to be told her duties, Mrs Everett paid her because she thought she'd need the money."

"I see. I think – I'd be glad if you can keep it that way, Miss Bowden. Not, for instance, give Mrs Everett any inkling that you've – spoken to the police."

"Yes. Of course. And all she can want from me are the

facts of what I found." And, if Phyllida played it right, a listening post. "I'm not looking forward to telling her, but if I make her cry it may help her to bear it."

"Yes. . . ." Kendrick had cried, in the solitude of the night, when Miriam had left him, but it hadn't seemed to help. His situation, though, had been different, Miriam had chosen to go. . . . "I'll appreciate it, Miss Bowden, if you'll see me again when you've seen Mrs Everett. It could be that she'll find herself more – relaxed – with her cleaning lady than with the police. Say, tomorrow?" The Chief Superintendent opened the leather-bound book on his desk.

"Tomorrow. Yes." Phyllida would like to have said today, and a final goodbye to Mrs Cookson by bedtime, but the Chief Superintendent was clearly dog-tired and probably on his way home when he had seen her out. "Could it be morning?" she asked. "I'm . . ." She had started to say on a reflex that she would be in the Snaith Gallery in the afternoon as he knew, but of course he refused to know, and she had made her decision not to force the truth on to him.

"I was going to suggest the morning." Kendrick's pen hovered above the open book. "Eleven o'clock?"

"I'll be here at eleven."

"Thank you, Miss Bowden." It was a common belief that one got used to taking unpleasant medicine, but Kendrick hadn't begun to get used to the unique substance which comprised Peter Piper's female operatives, although at least he was managing to be grimly amused by the strategy. "And now – I'm sure you want to be on your way to The Cedars."

Maurice Kendrick was more subtle than was superficially evident, even to someone as perceptive as Phyllida, a state of affairs which had served him well over the years, and when the door had closed on Miss Bowden the weariness her presence had apparently wrought in him disappeared and his eyes glittered as he turned to Detective Sergeant Wetherhead.

"That file again, please, sergeant!"

Sergeant Wetherhead placed in front of him one of the folders that had been removed from the locked drawer of David Lester's filing cabinet. It contained just one sheet of A4 paper on which was printed the name Paul Fisher and an address and telephone number in south London, above the word *Winter* and a series of dates, the last of which was the date of *Winter*'s arrival at the Snaith Gallery. The printout had come from the simple word processor on Lester's desk, which the experts had carted off, plus software, to discover if they would yield further information. Thelma Royle had told them an office door could be closed without inviting comment, to indicate its occupant didn't want to be disturbed unless it was urgent. "Say they've a client who asks for privacy, or a confidential phone call, or they really need to concentrate."

"You're ready, sergeant?" Kendrick was already dismantling the hierarchy of suspicion he had begun to create from the Gallery staff.

"Ready, sir?"

"To drive me to London."

"Tonight?"

"This very moment, Fred."

Phyllida went first to the Golden Lion to collect her car, which she left as usual in the empty circle at the top of the lane off Marlborough Drive. Mrs Everett must have been looking out for her, she appeared in the front doorway when Mrs Cookson was only halfway across the forecourt. Phyllida was shocked by her ravaged face, while at the same time somehow satisfied to see the first evidence of true mourning for David Lester.

"Ah, Mrs Cookson, how very kind of you! Please

come in." Mrs Everett's voice had lost its confidence and was softer in tone. She took Mrs Cookson's coat and herself hung it on a peg in the cloakroom, before leading the way to her small sitting-room. "There was a great deal of damage and disturbance everywhere as you know, but the police have finished in here and I've tried to put it to rights." Phyllida thought she had managed pretty well, although the injury to the little bureau was glaringly apparent. "My first thought was to stay at the Golden Lion for a time, but I find I can't leave this poor stricken place . . ." Mrs Everett choked to a halt, and motioned to Mrs Cookson with a handkerchief she was holding to take the chair opposite the one into which she was collapsing.

"Let it come," Mrs Cookson urged. "You cry, madam, it'll do you good."

"Oh, I have cried, and I'll cry again, but not now, not while you're here and I have the chance to talk to you." Mrs Everett gulped and blew her nose, managing a half smile as she put the handkerchief into her handbag. "Mrs Cookson . . . I'm so sorry you had to – find him." Phyllida saw the knuckles whiten as Mrs Everett tightened her grip on the handle of the bag. "But at the same time I'm grateful. That it wasn't me."

"Of course you are, and I'm glad I could spare you." Phyllida leaned forward. "'e'd of died right away, you know, no doubt of that."

Mrs Everett nodded. "That's what the police said, and it's something I'm grateful for. If he'd fought for his life. . . ." Mrs Everett closed her eyes and took a long quivering breath.

"You don't 'ave to think of that because it didn't 'appen. I know it's a funny kind of a thing to say, but 'e looked reelly peaceful. "'e didn't know what'd 'appened, 'e just – went on being asleep." It was the

108

best Phyllida could do, and she saw in Mrs Everett's face that it had been of help.

"I know. I had to – identify him." The eyes closed again. "It was the worst moment of my life, waiting for that sheet to go back, and then – yes, he did look peaceful. Oh, God!"

The crumpling of her face from its partial recovery was a disturbing sight. "So 'e wasn't killed 'cos he was trying to stop the burglary," Mrs Cookson diverted swiftly. "If it was a burglary. I dunno, 'cos of not 'aving 'ad time, reelly, to see what there is 'ere. Was anything taken?"

Mrs Everett nodded as she blew her nose. "A few small valuables," she said, after a short struggle. "A gold watch of mine, and David's Rolex, which was by his bed. . . ." Again she rallied. "My pearls. A couple of small silver things. All stuff that could be carried on the person. There may be more, I couldn't think. . . . No papers of mine seem to be missing, although like David's, they were gone through. Whether David lost any papers I wouldn't know, our household responsibilities were as separate as our lives. I feel very frustrated that I can't tell the police what, if anything, is missing from among David's things."

"They'll 'ave the second anonymous letter. It's lucky you give it to Dr Piper."

"Is it?" Mrs Everett asked bitterly. "Lucky to have given them false evidence against him?" She stopped abruptly, recollecting her audience.

"Against someone," Phyllida amended automatically. She had just had an unpleasant thought of her own. "I 'ope you realise, Mrs Everett, as 'ow I wouldn't of been daft enough to take any of your or Mr Lester's things when I found 'e was dead. I'm honest as it 'appens, but if I wasn't, working for Dr Piper I'd 'ave been a prize fool."

Mrs Everett looked genuinely startled. "I never thought of it, Mrs Cookson. In the circumstances, I have to say. But of course I accept your statement that you are honest."

In the circumstances, Phyllida thought ruefully, that was easy enough. "Thank you, madam."

Mrs Everett's thoughts were already elsewhere. "Mrs Cookson. . . ."

"Yes, madam?" For the moment Phyllida could read those thoughts as easily as if she could see them. Mrs Everett was struggling between her longing to defend her brother and her inbred sense of the proprieties. "You talk to me, now, if you feel the need. I know you wouldn't, normal like, but things ain't normal and you and I do share a secret."

"Oh, yes, we do, Mrs Cookson, that's really why I so wanted to see you!" Phyllida had brought the barrier down. "I'm so – so bewildered. So angry! Mr Carrington came to see me just now – he's the director of the gallery where David works – worked" – Phyllida was shocked by the great dry sob – "and he came to tell me – what was threatened in those terrible letters. The third Sandys picture – *Winter* – has turned out to be a fraud, and he said – he meant it kindly, he was warning me – he said it's going to seem that David was guilty. David! My brother couldn't perpetrate a fraud if he tried, he was pathologically honest!" Mrs Everett's choice of vocabulary showed Phyllida she had secured her hoped-for role of listening-post. "And if he'd done something wrong, why would he have been killed, that's what I want to know! The only reason David could have been murdered . . ." Mrs Everett paused and closed her eyes again, and Phyllida saw her jaw tighten as if she was biting on the bitter kernel of her loss. ". . . is if he knew someone else was guilty and they were afraid of exposure. And by killing him the person guilty of the

110

fraud could put the blame on him because he isn't here now to defend himself. That's right, isn't it? Isn't it, Mrs Cookson?"

"Unless the murder was nothing to do with the fraud, madam."

Mrs Everett's lapsing animation was re-aroused. "Of course it was to do with the fraud! There was nothing else in David's life that could possibly. . . . I told the police, I told them . . . Since his marriage broke up, David's lived for his work, and to help me keep a good home."

"No '*chercher lar farme*', then?" Mrs Cookson suggested archly.

"No . . .?" Repugnance came with interpretation. "Indeed not!" Mrs Everett reprimanded. "David has never – played about with women. Never! He was very badly affected by the break-up of his marriage, and in any case it isn't – wasn't – oh, God – in his nature to philander. There is only one explanation for his death, Mrs Cookson. He found out about the fraud at the Gallery, and he paid the price."

"That's terrible." Mrs Cookson shook her head in astonishment. "If that's the case, it's terrible."

"It is the case," Mrs Everett said firmly. Whether she felt as firm in her mind as she appeared in her attitude, Phyllida was unable to read. But she could see that Mrs Everett would school herself in her expressed belief, as the way to enable her to carry on. "I am, of course, happy to have paid you for the full week, Mrs Cookson," she ended.

"Thank you, madam. And I'm sorry I can't 'elp you no more. But when I said that to Dr Piper 'e give me to understand . . . 'e's doing something at the Gallery?"

"That's right," Mrs Everett said dismissively. What happened at the Gallery was no concern of Mrs Cookson's, and so she got to her feet. Just one day of supreme grief

111

seemed to have turned her elegant curves into angles and her face looked pinched and almost plain. Phyllida felt a pang of pity, and put out a hand as she, too, rose.

It came to rest on Mrs Everett's where it still clutched the handbag, and was not repulsed. "I wish I could 'ave done more for you, I reelly do."

"You did all you could." The response was mechanical; Mrs Everett was already occupied with the problem of how to cope with the solitude which would follow Mrs Cookson's departure.

Feeling subdued, Phyllida returned to her car and drove to the car park at the back of the Golden Lion. All she wanted in the world was to shed Mrs Cookson and take her own self across the road to bring the team up to date over mugs of coffee. But when she paused to glance into the lobby bar, as she always did between coming through from the back door and setting foot on the back stairs, she saw Mr Brooke sitting alone with a glass, his face in profile, fixed on the entrance.

"Any messages for Mrs Sunbury?" she asked on the telephone, the moment she was in her room.

"No, madam." All the reception staff, at all times, called her madam, and Phyllida reckoned they must be grateful for the all-encompassing sobriquet.

She pulled off Mrs Cookson's hair and tossed it on to the bed. Mr Brooke's presence in the Golden Lion might have nothing to do with Mrs Sunbury, he might be waiting for someone else to join him or be about to leave, but she had to put herself in the way of an encounter. She rang down to Reception and asked them to let her know immediately if the gentleman she was about to describe to them left the hotel. Then, allowing herself an audible groan, she began the change that must by-pass the self she was longing to return to after as bizarre a day as she remembered spending. When she was half way there she rang across the square and told Peter why she couldn't make it. He assured her he would be in his office at whatever time she could.

Fifteen minutes later Anita Sunbury strolled into the lobby bar and up to the counter. When she had ordered and obtained a dry martini she turned and idly surveyed the tables, nodding amiably and without surprise towards Mr Brooke. He got immediately to his feet and she sauntered across to his table with her drink in her hand.

"Six o'clock spot on," she said, looking up at the big clock over the bar. "I thought I was starting my evening's drinking pretty promptly, but you're there before me."

"Won't you sit down?" Mr Brooke asked her.

"If you're not expecting anyone else I shall be delighted to."

"I'm not expecting anyone. Living alone I tend to enjoy an early evening drink at an agreeable hostelry on my way home."

But he hadn't found the Golden Lion agreeable for the past few months, unless she had missed his every visit. "You didn't leave the Gallery today, then, when the police told us we could go?"

"No. I stayed on with Mr Carrington and Thelma while they started the process of coming to terms. And there are some practical considerations, as you may imagine."

"Of course." Phyllida sat down.

Mr Brooke surveyed her quizzically, still armoured in his ironic self-possession. "Well, Mrs Sunbury, how do I find you? You've been at the Snaith Gallery just three days, and tomorrow it will be a headline in every national newspaper. You've had to give a statement to the police, and you may find yourself a media target at any moment. Are you bearing up?"

"I hope so, Mr Brooke. Are you?"

"I hope so."

"Do tell me," Mrs Sunbury drawled, leaning back at her most relaxed. "Have you a theory?"

113

"I have an anger!" Mr Brooke's serene blue eyes were all at once flashing fire. Phyllida gave a physical start before she could think of controlling it. "This isn't a crime story, Mrs Sunbury, a good man has died!"

"I'll take your word for that, Mr Brooke. And any man's death diminishes us, as John Donne said. I am *not* being facetious," Anita finished seriously.

"No, of course not, forgive me. I am well aware that your sort of person responds to my sort as a challenge." The perception was spot on, and Mr Brooke had resumed his detached stance. "But there are times and situations when the game grows tawdry."

"I'm glad you see it that way." Anita nestled comfortably into the small chair as Phyllida decided she liked Mr Brooke better than she had thought she could. "Seriously, do you have any ideas about David Lester's death?"

"I have to believe it has to do with the Sandys forgery. But that doesn't mean I have to believe David perpetrated it. If he'd taken his own life. . . . But he was murdered. What does that suggest to *you*, Mrs Sunbury?"

"It suggests," Phyllida said slowly, "that someone was running scared of what he knew, what he could say, and decided to shut him up." It was Mrs Everett's theory, and it made the most sense. Especially when one thought about the man or woman who had actually painted *Winter*. "And of course—"

"Exactly. Someone decided to shut him up. Mrs Sunbury—"

"We mustn't forget the person who painted *Winter*. He or she could have been afraid of what David Lester knew."

"David couldn't have known anything about the forger if he wasn't responsible for the forgery!" The flash was briefly back in the blue eyes. "And he wasn't."

"You know that?"

"I know – I knew – David!"

114

She was not going to get anywhere on that tack. "You knew him well, Mr Brooke?"

The eyes were hooded, sliding down to the table. "Well enough, through a working association, to recognise his honesty. It was easy to recognise. You spoke to him, didn't you, Mrs Sunbury, I saw you in his office doorway on Tuesday. Only Tuesday. . . ." Mr Brooke mused into his glass, and a shudder went through him which Phyllida could see was involuntary.

"Yes. He very kindly offered to photostat the catalogues of the two Sandys exhibitions for me. I thought he seemed a nice man, but I'm hardly in a position to pass a moral judgment. I also thought – he seemed worried and jumpy."

"Yes," Mr Brooke conceded, Phyllida thought reluctantly. "David hasn't been his usual cheerful self of late. But so much hung for him on the verdict on the last of the Sandys pictures."

"I would have thought that by this stage he would have been comparatively relaxed about it, having received two favourable opinions."

"But the third one wasn't favourable, was it, Mrs Sunbury? Now . . ." Mr Brooke looked at his watch. "I should like to buy you your second drink, but I'm afraid I have to get home, I have a visitor arriving. Another time, I hope. But perhaps I might just say something before I go. . . . In your interests, Mrs Sunbury."

"In my interests? That sounds rather worrying."

"I hope not. But – Philip Morgan. . . ."

"Philip Morgan?"

"He's a violent man, Mrs Sunbury. I think you should bear that in mind."

"You know it from experience?"

Another shudder. "I know it. And I suspect he is also unscrupulous." Mr Brooke looked her steadily in the eyes.

"And why should you think that will be of concern to me, Mr Brooke?"

His eyes didn't waver. "Because I have noticed that you are attracted to one another. I am asking you merely to – remember what I have said."

"Thank you."

"And now I must leave you. Another time. . . ."

"Another time." Anita smiled her slow smile at him as he got to his feet, and Phyllida noted that it was without the power to prevent the sudden unveiling of age and tiredness in his face. Another mask torn off by the tragedy of David Lester's death. As she watched the tall, frail figure float into the revolving door, Phyllida wondered if Edward Brooke had really needed to leave, or had been as afraid of Mrs Sunbury's insight as she herself had initially been of his.

"I should have had whisky," she said to Peter, as he gestured towards his cabinet.

"No problem. There's more here than meets the eye from your side of the desk. Tonic or martini with the gin?"

"Better make it tonic. Thanks. I'm sorry about Steve and Jenny."

"So were they. Both had dates, or they'd still be here. And Brooke was still there when Anita came down. That was a bonus."

"So I thought at first. But as we talked I began to wonder if he'd put himself in the way of our meeting. If he does stop off for a drink on his way home, the Golden Lion certainly isn't on his regular list of hostelries. And. . . ."

"Yes?"

"I felt there was a sub-text. Well, several. Edward Brooke wanted to teach, and he wanted to learn. The teaching was interesting: he told Anita to beware of

116

Philip Morgan and no, I'm pretty sure it wasn't sexual jealousy. He said Philip was violent, that was his word, and probably unscrupulous as well. Don't ask me whether he was telling her this so that she could protect herself, or merely making a point, I don't know."

"Um. Interesting, as you say. Any more lessons?"

"On David Lester's honesty, and role as silenced scapegoat. Brooke's theory matches Mrs Everett's – Lester set up as responsible for the forgery, and then silenced so that he can't defend himself – and mine. Oops! I don't have one, do I?"

"No." They grinned at one another. "And the learning?" Peter asked.

"He'd noticed me speaking to David Lester in his office on Tuesday, the time when Lester offered to photostat the Sandys exhibitions for me. I think he wanted to know what we'd talked about. I suppose he could be sleuthing on his own account, or have some reason for being afraid of what Lester might have been saying to me, I just don't know. But I don't think we met by chance. When he was telling me Lester was innocent he went so fiercely serious he made me jump, so perhaps that was the main purpose of our encounter."

"But why bother?"

"A sense of fair play?"

"Most motives, I've found in this business, are less altruistic. How did you get on with the Detective Chief Superintendent?"

"Better than he got on with me – or rather, with Mary Bowden's voice and Mrs Cookson's appearance. He wasn't enjoying what was obviously an unfamiliar role as suppliant, needing Mary Bowden and wishing he didn't. I'm to go back in the morning – both of us wished it wasn't necessary – to tell him how Mrs Cookson got on with Mrs Everett."

"And how did she?"

"Interestingly, again."

"She rang me, you know, Mrs Everett," Peter said. "Wants me to carry on investigating, both on the personal and work side . . . no expense spared. Good for us."

"The burglary's unlikely to be a blind," Peter went on. "Seeing that Lester was killed in his sleep and there's no way the murderer could plead self-defence. It has to have been opportunist."

"Or an attempt to present the murderer as the sort of person he or she isn't?"

Peter was intrigued. "That's quite an insight."

"Perhaps. But they're bound to run the forger to earth sooner or later, and surely he – or she – will lead back to the murderer?"

"Or be the murderer."

"It's a more direct route than Anita Sunbury can take. But Mr Kendrick wants her to carry on."

"So do I. Another drink?"

"No, thanks. I've decided to go home tonight and I've got the car." The prospect was deeply consoling. "Golden Lion Reception will let me know if I need to make a call. I'm not seeing the Chief Superintendent until eleven, so it's worth while. Unless of course you want me to—"

"I want you to go home and stay there until it's time to give Mrs Cookson's farewell performance."

"Thanks." Phyllida paused when she was on her feet. "Peter, Mrs Everett was so certain her brother had no involvement with a woman. Which makes the profile even more intriguing. If only I'd seen her full face. Put it with the bracelet David Lester was so anxious to get out of his house, and it could be the key to everything."

"Or a red herring. Go home now and be Phyllida Moon householder until the morning."

Chapter Nine

Hartshorn Mews SW12 was a narrow crack even by mews standards, and Detective Sergeant Wetherhead had nosed past it when Kendrick's craning head saw the sign. It was half-past seven in the evening and a bunch of teenagers was lounging against the wall to both sides of the mouth of the mews, so close to each other in the slim space that only a murmur of voices came to the policemen through the open window of their car.

If they had turned in they would have squashed or scattered the group, and Wetherhead parked on the road. The car was unmarked, and the detectives in their usual lounge suits, but as they bisected the gathering two of the boys grinned and held out their hands as if inviting handcuffs. DS Wetherhead looked uneasy, but Kendrick grinned back and received a good-natured slow hand-clap.

"Number 7A?" he inquired.

"You're the Bill, ain't you?" one of the girls counter-questioned.

"Number 7A?" Sergeant Wetherhead repeated.

"Fourth on the left, first floor," the girl said. The lack of an answer to their question seemed to have satisfied the group they'd got it right.

"Thanks," Kendrick said, with another grin. He felt the collective and mildly curious gaze on his back as he and his sergeant walked on, both struggling slightly to keep a dignified steady pace on the prominent cobbles.

No historic property appeared to have been demolished

in Hartshorn Mews, but nor did any action appear to have been taken to preserve their decaying charms.

"A time capsule," Kendrick murmured, as they approached the indicated building. The single, original, door was marked both 7 and 7A, and when DS Wetherhead pushed it it opened on to a small lobby with an obviously modern front door immediately ahead, beside a steep, narrow staircase. A tipsy figure 7 was nailed to the wall beside the door, and Kendrick and Wetherhead climbed the drugget-covered stairs, turning a right angle on their way to another front door in the same utilitarian mode as the internal one below and painted the same dilapidated white. The figure 7 had an A beside it. DS Wetherhead rang the bell.

Immediate sounds behind the door reassured them that their client was at home, so the waiting time generated in Kendrick merely his ever-ready irritation.

"Yes?" As the door eventually and slowly opened, Kendrick snapped down the old-fashioned raised light switch on the wall beside it. The harsh glare of the unshaded bulb overhead revealed that the young man peering through the chain-width gap had floppy brown hair and was slim and slight. His features were delicate and his face thin and pale with a small spot of colour in the centre of each cheek. Kendrick's penchant for Victorian fiction made him think the word *consumptive* before recollecting he was a century out of date.

"Mr Paul Fisher?"

"Yes. . . ."

"Open the door, will you please, Mr Fisher," Kendrick ordered shortly, bringing out his ID and aware of the movement of his sergeant beside him bringing out his. "Detective Chief Superintendent Kendrick of Seaminster CID. This is Detective Sergeant Wetherhead."

"How can I be sure . . . IDs can be faked!" The light was good enough to show the fear in the dark eyes, and Kendrick suspected bluster rather than prudence.

"You can telephone Seaminster CID," he said, unhesitating but gentler. "We can give you the number and you can check it with Directory Inquiries."

The young man hesitated a moment during which Kendrick and Wetherhead stood deadpan and motionless. Then he made a gesture of surrender and pushed the door to before opening it wide.

"That's all right, you'd better come in."

In the narrow hallway, where the drugget extended, there was an immediate strong smell of paint. Kendrick had dabbled as a young man, and had to withstand its agreeable associations.

"Is it about my car?" the young man asked, a gleam of hope showing in what Kendrick had already gratefully decided were expressive eyes. "I'll admit I—"

"Not about your car, sir, no," DS Wetherhead interrupted. "It's a rather more serious matter."

"More serious. . . . Come in here will you, please."

Kendrick decided Paul Fisher had invited them into his studio so that he could fall on to the sofa rather than the floor. It took him a few seconds after his collapse among the brightly coloured rugs and cushions to motion the policemen to the two old armchairs, similarly adorned.

"Thank you, sir." As he sat down Kendrick leaned forward. "Are you all right? Sergeant, I think some water." Kendrick in his turn motioned towards the sink that stood under the small, paint-splashed sash window. Serious daytime light, he saw, would come from the now navy-blue skylight slanting down one side of the pitched ceiling.

DS Wetherhead, who had quickly settled into his seat, hauled himself out of it and crossed the cluttered space. While he searched for a container that at least looked to be uncontaminated by paint, Kendrick and Fisher surveyed one another in silence.

"Thanks." The young man took the cup from the sergeant without pretence of not needing it, and drank deeply.

"Now," Kendrick said gently and untruthfully, when his sergeant was settled for the second time. "Some papers have come into my possession which reveal that you have recently painted a picture entitled *Winter* in the style of the Pre-Raphaelite artist Frederick Sandys, claiming it to be by Sandys."

"But . . ." Kendrick was intrigued to note that fear had been replaced by bewilderment.

"It's a brilliant achievement," Kendrick continued, "and if it hadn't been painted on a canvas and with materials not in use at the time Frederick Sandys was alive and working, it could very well have deceived the experts."

"I don't understand . . . Materials not in use. . . ." Paul Fisher's eyes pleaded with the policemen to be a bad dream and disappear.

"Modern materials," DS Wetherhead contributed relentlessly. "AD 1990, or thereabouts. Paints and canvas."

"The bastard!" Paul Fisher sprang to his feet, eyes blazing, fists clenched. It was the last reaction Kendrick had expected. "The ****ing bastard! He's put it all on to me!" The eyes rediscovered Kendrick and Wetherhead. "Yes, I painted *Winter*," Paul Fisher declared angrily. "To order. I did exactly as I was told, I carried out my part of the agreement. And he. . . ." The eyes closed, then snapped open. "I'll kill him for this. I'll kill him!"

"Haven't you got your tenses wrong, sir?" Kendrick gently suggested.

"What?" The snapping dark eyes came back again to the policemen.

"You say you'll kill him, future tense. But it's past tense, isn't it, sir? You killed him last night."

Edward Brooke had been right about one thing: the murder of David Lester was an item on the TV news Phyllida saw that evening, and on the front page of her newspaper next morning beside a head and shoulders photograph which gave her a pang because the face wore the eager, cheerful expression David's colleagues had called his norm and which she had never seen.

The headline was *'Art Expert Murdered in his Bed'*, and on page three there was a potted biography under a photograph of The Cedars, with a small inset of Mrs Everett looking the way she had looked the day before. Phyllida scanned both pieces for the words *Sandys* and *Winter*, imagining the even greater anxiety with which the Director of the Snaith Gallery and his staff would be going through similar motions, and was relieved to find that where the name *Sandys* occurred it was each time in the context of the authentication and sale of *Spring* and *Summer*. Detective Chief Superintendent Kendrick had kept his word, and no member of the staff or their loved ones – at least as yet – had been seduced by the opportunity for an exclusive.

Phyllida took her time getting up and spent an enjoyable hour pottering about her house, during which the prospect of assuming Mrs Cookson felt more and more like a chore and an irrelevance. She drove to the Golden Lion for the transformation.

At eleven-fifteen Detective Chief Superintendent Kendrick apologised perfunctorily for having kept her waiting. He looked tired and at the same time uncharacteristically exhilarated, and the current of suppressed excitement passing between him and his sergeant was palpable. He hurried Miss Bowden through her account of her last meeting with Mrs Everett, and even though

123

Phyllida was well aware it had yielded no real information, she had expected before seeing him that he would wring from it every drop he could.

So she was unsurprised when instead of dismissing her he leaned back in his chair and told her he had something important to say to her.

"Chief Superintendent?"

"Miss Bowden . . . I'm about to play fair with you, as I hope you've played fair with me."

"Of course." Phyllida thought with a guilty pang of the profile.

"And I'm speaking on the assumption that – you – know what – Dr Piper's employee at the Snaith Gallery knows."

It was the clearest indication yet of the Detective Chief Superintendent's inability to believe in a single Mary Bowden.

"That assumption is correct."

"Thank you. Now, a young man has been brought in who has confessed to painting the picture called *Winter* which the director of the Snaith Gallery told the police and his staff about yesterday, in a confidence which I trust is being respected." Phyllida nodded as the Chief Superintendent paused and cleared his throat. "He has not confessed to the murder of David Lester, and is in fact so far denying ever having met the murdered man or visited his house. We've informed Mr Carrington that the young man is helping us with our inquiries, and of his confession of responsibility for the artistic fraud." Kendrick paused again. "We've warned him that the young man is also laying claim to the painting of *Spring* and *Summer*, a warning he will no doubt pass on to his staff." *So I'm not doing the Peter Piper Agency any favours*, Phyllida added in her head.

"Thank you for being so frank with me, Chief Superintendent." As well as being aware that during the afternoon one of Dr Piper's Miss Bowdens would find out everything he had just told her, the Chief Superintendent could be seeing himself as laying an additional moral injunction upon that composite lady to be as frank in her turn.

"At a press conference this afternoon the media will be informed that a man is helping the police with their inquiries into the death of David Lester. Knowledge of the existence of the painting called *Winter* is not, as you will be aware" – Phyllida saw the flash of ironic doubt cross his eyes – "in the public domain, and at this stage of the investigation, at least, there is no requirement that it should enter it. So the promise of secrecy given to the Director of the Snaith Gallery by his staff and by the police should continue to be kept."

"Of course." Phyllida liked the Chief Superintendent's concern in the midst of a murder inquiry for the comparatively minor matter of the reputation of an art gallery – although it could be, of course, that he merely preferred for the moment not to deflect attention from the major crime. "Chief Superintendent, may I take it that you won't want to see Mrs Cookson again?"

"Probably not, Miss Bowden, probably not. But I shall appreciate it if she can be – available at some later stage of the investigation should developments make that desirable."

"Of course," Phyllida said again, getting hopefully to her feet and relieved to see the two policemen do likewise.

Chief Superintendent Kendrick cleared his throat again as Mrs Cookson turned towards the door. "I shall be available to Mrs Sunbury, Miss Bowden, at any time she feels she has discovered something I ought to know."

"Of course," Phyllida assured him for the third time. She could see that he was struggling with a humbling exercise he must be finding totally unfamiliar, and was impressed by the way he was handling it. When the door had closed on Mrs Cookson, Kendrick stood for a moment in silence, wrinkling his nose.

"Anything wrong, sir?"

"No, Fred, nothing." It had to be nothing, nothing beyond a crazy reaction to the crazy situation of the ubiquitous Miss Bowdens, to find the scent Mrs Cookson had left behind her conjuring up a mental picture of Mrs Sunbury. "Let's go, we've got a lot of persuading to do!"

Despite his elation, Kendrick was aware of a sense of unease he couldn't explain to himself as they returned to the interview room where Paul Fisher was awaiting them. The young man had given no answers to any of the questions put to him more than once during the early part of the night, and had confessed to nothing beyond the painting of *Spring*, *Summer* and *Winter*. And through his steadily increasing disarray, his denial of ever having met David Lester or visited his house had been as unwavering and unvaried as a tape recording.

One of Kendrick's DIs, who had assisted in the preliminary questioning and was known as a keen amateur psychologist, had respectfully suggested the young man was in shock and would probably be more useful after a few hours of sleep and solitary, during which he could "come back to himself" and contemplate the seriousness of his situation. Kendrick had reluctantly agreed.

With first light, two CID officers had gone up to London to question Fisher's neighbours and Kendrick was back at the station by eight, where he was greeted with the news that Fisher had called for help in the small hours and been visited by the police doctor.

"What the hell's wrong with him?" Kendrick shouted.

"Panic and low blood pressure, sir, as far as anyone can make out. The doctor's given him something and says he'll be fit for more questioning by mid-morning."

So the mid-morning visit of Miss-Bowden-as-Mrs-Cookson was something Kendrick could have done without, particularly as it yielded nothing to advance his progress on the murder case – he had heard Mrs Everett's theory from her own lips, and Carrington had told him he intended to call on her. But at least it got him over the uncomfortable business of passing on to Miss Bowden the information she would receive that afternoon from the director of the Snaith Gallery which he hoped, when his action was relayed to her boss, would result in Piper's encouragement of all the Mary Bowdens to be entirely frank with the police. . . .

Paul Fisher was slumped in the chair opposite Kendrick and Wetherhead, the two red spots in his cheeks even more prominent against their marble pale surround. Kendrick wondered if it was the spots that were responsible for his uneasiness. Perhaps Fisher did have TB; it was said to be coming back.

"Right!" he said briskly, as he sat down. "You feeling better, lad?"

"I'm all right." The continuous slight movement of his jaw showed that Fisher was grinding his teeth, and Kendrick was aware of a tension replacing the earlier loose-limbed collapse.

"Still sure you don't want a solicitor?"

"Still sure."

"Very well. Perhaps now you'll answer some questions." He motioned to his sergeant, who switched on the tape and recorded time and persons present. "That'll help you as well as us, you know."

"I don't need help. I've never met the man you say was murdered, and I've never been to his house."

"You've merely faked a picture or two."

"That isn't murder."

"No. Now, you've never been to David Lester's house, but you know his name." It was a shot to nothing.

127

"I know the name Lester," Fisher muttered, after a pause in which Kendrick and Wetherhead repeated their deadpan performance.

It was the first departure from the recording Fisher had played over and over to them the night before, and Kendrick had to suppress a glance of triumph at his sergeant.

"Lester?" DS Wetherhead asked. "Lord Lester? Mr Lester?"

"He called himself Lester on the telephone, no handle."

"Lester on the telephone," Kendrick repeated. "So someone calling himself Lester simply telephoned you one day and asked you to paint him some pictures?"

"Yes."

"Why did he do that?"

"Because he wanted something he could pass off as the real thing, and he knew that from me he'd get it. And I knew what I was doing, because he had to tell me why he wanted the pictures to make sure I kept quiet and destroyed all the evidence." Something of the defiance of the night before was back in the dark eyes. As Kendrick gazed back into them in silence, Fisher's mouth twisted into a pained half smile. "You don't remember, do you, Mr Kendrick? A couple of years ago I sold a pompous git of a gallery owner, who had rejected one of *my* pictures, a phoney Lord Leighton. When he'd made a fool of himself with it I owned up. The media got hold of it, and I sold some of my other copies. As copies. There was this critic said I was the best copier he'd come across. That's why Lester knew where to go."

Kendrick had a vague memory of the media jamboree. "It does appear that you're very good, Mr Fisher. Particularly if you painted all three of the so-called Sandys."

"I did."

"The Director of the Snaith Gallery doesn't agree

with you." But they were moving too far away from the murdered man. "So Lester always got in touch with you by telephone?"

"Yes. He said it was the safest way. And all the time he had me down on paper. Jesus. . . ." Kendrick saw the fury again, in the brief distortion of the face and the fist clenched on the edge of the table.

"But you must have been afraid of that, to turn his house over."

"I didn't turn his house over, I never even went to it!"

"All right. On the telephone . . . Did he have a distinctive voice?"

"You could say so. He used some distorting device, it wasn't normal, it was sort of – electronic."

"I see. Now, the night David Lester was killed. Wednesday. What did you do that night, Mr Fisher?"

"Nothing!" The defiance crumbled as the two policemen stared in silence. "Nothing," Fisher repeated, as a mutter.

"Nothing? You mean you were at home?"

Paul Fisher nodded.

"For the tape, sir," DS Wetherhead asked.

"Yes. I was at home."

"No visitors?"

"No."

"But I expect you made or received a telephone call or two?"

"I can't remember." The answer came pat. Kendrick suspected Fisher of having rehearsed his apology for an alibi.

"That's a pity," he commiserated. "But perhaps you watched TV?"

Fisher nodded.

"For the tape," the detective sergeant repeated.

"I watched a thing about animals in Africa. Half-past eight, nine o'clock, some time like that."

"I see, sir." Reports of the murder hadn't appeared in the media until after Fisher had been taken in, and Kendrick had issued a stern injunction to everyone at Police HQ that he was to be denied access to radio or newspaper and despite Fisher's pleas, had stuck to it himself during the unsatisfactory first stage of the interrogation the night before. So, if Fisher was innocent, he didn't know what part of Wednesday night he needed cover for, and if he was guilty but smart he would act as though he didn't. In either case an animal programme would be a good choice because it wouldn't have a story and he'd be safe, if he hadn't actually watched it, to say it had contained sex and violence. . . . All a waste of effort, Kendrick thought on a surge of mingled triumph and exasperation, in view of the information provided by another of Dr Piper's field workers.

"You can check. And then, when I couldn't sleep, I watched a film. Something about twin sisters, a goodie and a baddie. Must have been one o'clock in the morning by the time it finished." Kendrick let out a long relieved breath. "I dozed through half of it."

"Thank you, sir. And then you went to bed."

"Yes."

"So you're telling me that between say 1.30 and 7.30 a.m. you were asleep."

"Off and on."

"And David Lester was killed between 12.30 and 7.30 a.m. It wouldn't take much more than an hour to drive from London to Seaminster during the night. That left you plenty of time, Mr Fisher."

"Damn you for a sadist!" Fisher had leaped to his feet, but quickly wavered and fell back into his chair. If he was faking the shock he was doing it well. "I didn't kill him! I never even met him! For all I knew he was a syndicate."

130

"But he wasn't, Mr Fisher, he was a single human being who had his throat cut while he was asleep in bed." He had told Fisher this the night before, but the young man's hand flew to his own throat a second time as Kendrick repeated it and he made a choking sound. "Anyway, let's hope one at least of your neighbours will be able to confirm that you spent the night at home, they're being questioned at the moment. Take it easy now!" Kendrick added in alarm. Fisher had keeled over on to the table, but by the time DS Wetherhead was round it he was sitting up again and shrugging off the helping hands.

"I'm all right. But I've changed my mind. I want a solicitor. And I'm not going to say another word until he gets here."

Chapter Ten

Outside the doors of the Snaith Gallery at two o'clock, Mrs Sunbury had to run the gauntlet of a media jostle. Phyllida was relieved to coincide with a couple of visitors and be assumed to be a third – a media posse at the Golden Lion would be a grave abuse of John Bright's hospitality.

Inside the Gallery there were more visitors than she had yet seen, some of them not even pretending to look at the pictures.

Thelma was standing beside Deborah at the reception desk. "Vultures!" she hissed as Anita reached them. "We'd have done better staying closed today, but Mr Carrington has such a strong sense of duty. He'd like to see you, Anita, when you're ready."

"Fine, honey. You all all right?"

Thelma shrugged. "We've got to be, Mr Carrington's so magnificent."

"The police have arrested someone already!" Deborah said excitedly.

"Be quiet, Deborah! And they haven't *arrested* anyone." Thelma's voice had sunk to a whisper. "They have someone helping them with their inquiries. I expect the Director will tell you, Anita, although it's something else he wants to see you about."

"Yes!" Deborah took up. "D'you know, that woman—"

"And we'll let Mr Carrington conduct his own business," Thelma reprimanded. "You really must keep

132

quiet, Deborah, it's called loyalty."

"Sorry!" Deborah offered both women an apologetic smile. "I do understand. And about the paintings. I know—"

"We know you do. And that even when we don't think anyone else can hear we still don't talk. All right?"

"Yes. Sorry," Deborah repeated, at last subsiding.

"I'm on my way," Anita said.

It felt absurd, to tap on a section of Gallery wall then wait and listen like a woodpecker, and Phyllida found herself looking round to make sure there was no one observing her. When the wall moved inwards she almost fell into the gap.

"It *is* disconcerting at first." Mr Carrington was smiling as he urged her inside and closed the gap behind her. When the smile faded she saw that yesterday's fitful ravagement of his face had become today's norm. "Please sit down, Mrs Sunbury."

"Thank you." Anita sank gracefully to the sofa.

"There are two reasons why I've asked to see you." The director remained on his feet, as he had done at their first private meeting, but Phyllida could see that this time the marble chimney piece was taking his weight. And this time the grey patio was already dark with rain, which might serve to thin out the media ranks. "I want to tell you what I told the other members of staff this morning following a further visit from Detective Chief Superintendent Kendrick, and I want to ask you if you'll reconsider your decision to work in the Gallery part-time only. The young woman appointed for the mornings has decided this is not the place for her, and gave in her notice on the telephone today at half-past nine." The strong, tired face twisted into an ironic smile. "Before I make any other move to fill the vacancy, I'm offering it again to you, Mrs Sunbury. I've already gathered you get on well with the public and the other members of staff, something I'm horribly afraid could be particularly important in the days to come, and that you're very ready to build on your existing knowledge of the art world. So – will you reconsider?"

Anita Sunbury smiled up at him. "You know, Mr Carrington, sometimes fate's timing can be exquisite. Last night I saw my doctor, and he told me my recovery has been so rapid I'm quite well enough again to work a full day. So I was regretting having opted for afternoons only." Anita spread her arms in pleased surrender to fate, and the Director's smile for an instant reached his eyes.

"That's good news, Mrs Sunbury. From tomorrow, then?"

"From tomorrow. Thank you for giving me a second chance. And now, you said. . . . ?"

"I've told the other members of staff what the Chief Superintendent had to say this morning, so now I must tell you. The police have a young man assisting them with their inquiries into David Lester's murder. He's denying having anything to do with the killing, but he claims he painted *Winter*." Mr Carrington closed his eyes for a moment, then squared his shoulders. "Well, we knew it was a forgery, we've already bitten on *that* bullet. The Chief Superintendent was good enough to tell me that, so far, no evidence of the man's work on the picture has been found – no preliminary sketches, palette with the paint range, and so on – and he and I agree this could be consistent with guilt as well as innocence: a forger would hardly retain the material that could convict him of his forgery."

"Hardly, no. *Spring* and *Summer*?" Phyllida ventured.

"Ah!" The Director flung himself into the pale gold armchair at right angles to the sofa. "The forger of *Winter* is insisting he forged *Spring* and *Summer* as well, but there's no evidence in his studio of that either, and no reason to believe him. The materials are right, and the pictures reached us in quick succession. *Winter* came after a much longer gap, and it's my personal belief that Sandys got round to painting only the first three seasons and – someone – was unable to resist producing the fourth."

"You yourself. . . ." Anita began, as the animation generated by his solacing thesis faded from the director's face. "With all your experience, do you yourself feel *Spring* and *Summer* are right?"

The question was an impertinence, but Phyllida had already been intrigued to notice that the fact of Mrs Sunbury being American appeared to make acceptable what would be considered an intrusion by a fellow-native. Mr Carrington was even smiling. "I do, Mrs Sunbury. I totally share the conviction of the experts I consulted."

"Then they're safe," Mrs Sunbury declared. "Even if the scandal of *Winter* gets out."

"Which it will." The smile now was weary. "Even if this young man is found to have no connection with the murder, he has confessed to the forgery of *Winter*, which means its existence will inevitably become public knowledge. As will his insistence that he painted *Spring* and *Summer* as well. Not that I'm afraid of *that*. No evidence will be found, and the claim will be seen for what it has to be. Vanity."

"I'm sure you're right!" Phyllida was surprised and amused by her own leap of heart on behalf of the stricken giant trying to rally in front of her. "And meanwhile, I'm sure you can rely on your staff, the existence of *Winter* won't trickle out as gossip. And maybe it won't come out at all if the forger's charged with murder."

"So doth the greater outrage dim the less." The smile reached the eyes again. "To misquote our greatest poet. Oh, it will come out, it will have to. But I think the

135

Gallery, as well as *Spring* and *Summer*, will be able to withstand it."

"I'm sure it will!" She had pushed her luck far enough for the moment, and Anita got to her feet. "Thank you so much, Mr Carrington, for offering me the full-time job, I'm very pleased to take it."

"And I'm very pleased you feel able to. Don't hesitate to come to me, Mrs Sunbury, if there's anything at all to do with your work here that you'd like to talk about."

"I won't." Phyllida was interested to find herself aware that, although the director of the Snaith Gallery clearly approved of Mrs Sunbury, his invitation was precisely what it seemed, free of sexual sub-text. And, alone with him behind his unmarked door, she had no sense of her own self as a safety net into which Anita *in extremis* could escape, a sense that was with her constantly in the company of Philip Morgan, even in public. . . . "Thank you, Mr Carrington."

He had walked past her, was opening his door. "Thank *you*, Mrs Sunbury."

Thelma was standing there, her hand raised to knock. "I'm sorry to disturb you, Mr Carrington, but the CID are here again and would very much like a further word with you."

"Ask them if they'll be good enough to come to my office then, Thelma."

"Yes, of course. I'll go and— Ah!" Detective Chief Superintendent Kendrick had made his own way from Reception and was standing behind her.

"I'm sorry to disturb you again, Mr Carrington," Kendrick said in his usual grave way, "but we've received some information I'm hoping you may be able to help us to interpret." DS Wetherhead appeared beside him.

"Of course, Chief Superintendent, anything I can do." Anita Sunbury's characteristic quizzical gaze was enabling Phyllida to look searchingly into the Director's face and find there no more than curiosity. "Please come in."

As the door closed Thelma looked anxiously at Phyllida. "This is a terrible ordeal for him!"

"For everyone, honey. Thelma, I'm going to work at the Gallery full time!"

"Oh, I am glad!" When Thelma smiled her mouth turned up and her cheeks dimpled, suggesting a sense of fun not normally in evidence.

"So am I!"

Phyllida wondered as she strolled towards Reception if she would still be glad had her job at the Snaith Gallery been what it seemed. One of the intriguing things about her second career was the way it enabled her to taste careers she had missed out on. So far, she had no regrets.

The main gallery was milling with people, and throughout the afternoon a steady stream approached the desk to ask directly or indirectly about David Lester. At one point Pamela Bennett shouted a protest, attracting more, and Anita and Deborah dealt with the crowd together until closing time. Several people expressed their anger at the police for not having made an immediate arrest and Phyllida hugged her anonymity and felt sorry for the Chief Superintendent, whose face was already nationally known.

As the Director of the Snaith Gallery closed the door that appeared to seal them into his room and turned with courteous expectancy to the policemen, Maurice Kendrick was inclined to feel sorry for himself.

"Please sit down, Chief Superintendent. Sergeant."

"Thank you, sir." Wetherhead lowered his stocky body gingerly to the sofa, and as Kendrick took one of the gold armchairs his distaste for his afternoon's brief did not blunt the keenness with which he was watching the Director of the Snaith Gallery and noting the lack of anxiety or reserve with which the deep-set grey eyes met his. Charles Carrington had to be unaware of the bizarre alibi Paul Fisher had sullenly offered them after consulting with the duty solicitor. "Now, the young man helping us with our inquiries has told us he spent Wednesday night – the night David Lester was killed – at a flat in Seaminster."

Interest and nothing else, Kendrick could swear. "That doesn't look very good for him, does it, Mr Kendrick? Can you tell me whereabouts in Seaminster the flat is?"

"Yes. It's in a block on the promenade on the corner of Leinster Road. It's called Ocean View and it's owned by you."

"What?" Amazement pure and simple, he'd swear again. "Ocean View? I don't understand . . . Ocean View does belong to me, I was a member of the syndicate that built it and afterwards the others pulled out and I became sole owner. I don't understand," Carrington said again. "You're saying the man you're questioning claims to have stayed in one of my flats the night David was killed?"

"He is, sir. After consultation with a solicitor. He didn't want one at first, but when I told him his neighbours in London were being asked if they could confirm he was at home that night, he asked for the solicitor, and following advice he told us he'd spent the night in Flat Number Three at Ocean View."

"Flat Number Three . . . Dear God." Carrington flung himself into the other armchair and buried his face in his hands.

"Sir?" Kendrick ventured, after a few moments of alternately exchanging looks with his sergeant and admiring the fireplace.

Carrington removed his hands and gazed wide-eyed at Kendrick. "Chief Superintendent. . . . There's no point in trying to keep it from you. And he's dead, I can't harm him further. Flat Number Three was rented last summer for a few weeks by David Lester's sister, Mrs Everett, for her son and his family. David did the business with me, and I gave him the key."

"Which he presumably gave back to you when the letting was over?"

"Of course. But. . . ."

"Keys are easily cut, yes. But since then . . . Has the flat been unlet since the summer?"

"It could have been, I'm afraid too many of them are once the season's over. But Flat Three was taken soon after Mrs Everett's family left – I can't remember precisely when that was – on an indefinite lease. I do remember feeling pleased at the time, but if it meant—"

"Would you know if the flat's been occupied throughout the current lease?"

Carrington spread his hands, trying to smile. "I'm afraid not. I'm an absentee landlord, Mr Kendrick, and I leave the day-to-day business to my agent Tom Jenkins. But even he may not be sure of the times the flat has been actually occupied – all the flats are let very adequately furnished, so it isn't immediately obvious whether or not a lessee is resident there, and although Tom has a master key, he wouldn't enter a flat uninvited unless there was something obviously wrong. I go there myself only if summoned for a specific reason and, say, two or three times a year to get the feel of how things in the building are generally. Tom will give you what information he can, I'll let you have his address and telephone number before you go." Carrington got to his feet and stood looking down at Kendrick. "Chief Superintendent, I'm not taking this in. You've told me a young man has claimed to have spent the night in one of my flats. Has he told you why, and how he got in?"

"He got in with a key which is now in police possession. And he says he went there because a man who called himself Lester – just Lester – had sent him the key, told him to spend that particular night there. According to the young man, Lester indicated he would join him at some point during his stay, and the young man wanted the encounter." *And another commission*, Kendrick added silently, remembering the anger in Fisher's eyes, the reclenched fist, when he told them Lester had also said on the telephone that there would be no more work. "The young man also told us Lester had sent him the key a long time before he issued his overnight invitation. That he sent it in early September, in time for the young man to deliver the painting *Spring* to Flat Three."

"No living artist had anything to do with *Spring*!" It was the first reaction beyond bewilderment Carrington had shown since Kendrick's revelation. He started pacing the room. "He may have delivered *Winter* as he says, but not *Spring* or *Summer*!"

"He claims to have painted and delivered the three. But I can tell you, Mr Carrington, that the papers removed from Mr Lester's files refer only to *Winter*."

"Thank you for telling me, Mr Kendrick, I appreciate it. But that's all they could refer to." Carrington spoke as a man justified in his faith rather than given cause to believe. "The young man simply jumped on an attractive and accessible bandwagon. If he was good enough to paint *Winter* and be rumbled only because he used anachronistic materials, it would be pretty tempting." Carrington flung himself back into his chair. "May I ask if he told you any details about the delivery of *Winter*?"

"He told us he delivered each picture" – Kendrick chose his words with deliberate provocation, and noted the flash of furious disbelief that crossed the Director's face – "on a Sunday evening, to an empty cupboard in the smaller of the two bedrooms. He said the flat was always empty and without evidence of recent occupation – no perishables in the fridge, no clothes in the drawers – but clean and tidy. His telephone instructions for Wednesday night were to get there by ten p.m. and make up his own bed – he says he found bedclothes as directed, and that there were tea and coffee and the basics for breakfast. And TV, which he watched." If Fisher was now telling the truth, the animal programme would have been on while he was in transit. "He maintains no one came and that he left at eight the next morning as instructed and went straight back to London."

"It's crazy." The director shook his head and offered both men his attractive rueful smile. "It's completely mad."

"We shall have to see, sir," DS Wetherhead said. "Do you remember the look of the packages containing the pictures? Was *Winter* packed and addressed in the same style as *Spring* and *Summer*?"

"I don't remember thinking there was any difference between them. In each case, brown paper, string, capital letters, which we of course examined when we discovered what was inside and that there was no explanation."

"Were the pictures registered?"

"No." Carrington shuddered. "I *do* remember feeling shocked about that. I even made a joke at the press conference following the authentication of *Summer*. I asked the anonymous donor to please insure *Winter* before posting it to us. Dear God." The director looked unhappily from Kendrick to Wetherhead, who made a vague effort to sit upright. "I suppose David – I'm sorry, I mean whoever it was – could have noted the wrapping and the form of address on the first two pictures, and copied it for the fake."

141

"That's possible. If it was someone who works at the Snaith Gallery. Did you by any chance retain any of the wrappings?"

"I *did* ask Thelma to keep the wrapping of *Winter* as a possible clue to the identity of the donor – by then we were really anxious to find him or her, if only to say thank you." Carrington closed his eyes again, and Kendrick saw his fists clench on the arm of his chair. "But it must have got caught up with wrapping from other packages and been thrown away, we never found it. Unless. . . ." Carrington stared large-eyed at Kendrick.

"Unless someone deliberately removed it." Kendrick put the thoughts of both of them into words as he got to his feet. "We won't keep you any longer now, Mr Carrington. If you'll just let me have the information about your agent for Ocean View."

"Yes, of course." Carrington got up and walked like an old man to the table behind the sofa, where he used the onyx pen projecting from an onyx base to write on the top sheet of a note pad in an onyx container. He tore it off and handed it to Kendrick. "He's a Seaminster man, you'll easily get hold of him. He'll be able to tell you the name of the lessee." Carrington shuddered. "All I remember of it is that it isn't Lester. Tom may not be able to tell you the times the flat's been occupied during the lease, but there can't have been anything going on in it to worry him or he'd have told me."

"What we've discussed this morning, sir," DS Wetherhead said as he and Kendrick followed the Director to the door, "we'll be obliged if you'll keep it to yourself for the time being."

"Of course." Carrington paused, his hand on his reticent door. "Chief Superintendent, may I ask you . . . Do you believe the young man spent Wednesday night in my flat?"

"We don't know, sir. But we do know he's been

142

there, his fingerprints are all over it. Thank you for your co-operation, Mr Carrington, we'll keep in touch."

When Kendrick went back through the main gallery, Mrs Sunbury was sitting behind the Reception desk beside the young girl he would have told to wash her face if she had been his daughter.

The woman they were talking to nudged her companion, staring at him, and he decided his pause would be brief. "Good afternoon, Mrs Sunbury."

"Chief Superintendent." To his reluctant gratitude she murmured his identity under her breath. "Do you want to speak with me?"

"Not at the moment." But to his annoyance, Kendrick found himself thinking as he walked briskly to the door how useful it might have been if one of Peter Piper's Miss Bowdens had been operating for the past week or two in the vicinity of Ocean View.

Chapter Eleven

"So," Philip Morgan said, when Mrs Sunbury had insinuated herself on to the adjacent bar stool at the New Caprice and he had bought her a dry martini. "The Snaith Gallery is to have the pleasure of your presence for the whole working day."

Anita gave her throaty chuckle. "Sonia's morning replacement didn't take long to decide she wasn't suited, did she?"

"It's a type. When it's at school it says, 'Please, miss, it wasn't me' whenever there's trouble. And when it grows up and sees a risk of trouble by association, it sends messages regretting it won't be around any more because something's cropped up."

"Sonia'll be relieved. She suspected the morning lady of nursing ambitions to become a permanency."

"And you don't?"

"Of course not," Anita said teasingly, and Phyllida knew she was already treading the fine line between dangerous provocation and the necessity of bringing as many reactions out of Philip Morgan as possible. "What do you take me for?"

"So it's get what you can out of a situation and then move on?"

"No. It's that I'm not looking for permanent employment."

Phyllida had put only a hint of chill into Anita's eyes, but Philip Morgan dropped his to the counter. "I'm sorry."

144

"Is it a bit of a habit with you, honey? Being confrontational?"

He looked up, met and held her gaze. "I don't know. If it is, it's a habit I haven't cultivated. And aren't you making a large assumption on a very small amount of evidence?"

"Now *I'm* sorry. I should have told you first about my encounter last night with Mr Brooke."

"You mean out of school?" His eyes were wary.

"Yes. In the bar at the Golden Lion. When I came down before dinner he was sitting on his own with a drink, and a newspaper he wasn't reading. I went over to him with my drink and he asked me to sit down. He made a point of telling me right away he was in the Golden Lion because of being in the habit of stopping off for a drink on his way home, but I've never seen him there before and I had the feeling he'd come hoping to meet me."

"Not for your *beaux yeux*. I'm sorry, that sounds ungallant, but I'll explain. First, though – why the feeling?"

"I think he wanted to impress on me that David Lester was innocent of the forgery. Not because I'm Anita Sunbury, just because he wants to impress it on everyone. He was so passionate about it I got a shock – I'd only seen him till that moment totally laid back and detached. He seems to think very highly of Mr Lester. Were they good friends?"

"Edward would have liked them to be, on his special terms. He's gay, Anita. In fairness, I think he fell for David the person as well as David the potential sex partner, and I know – I think we all know – how kindly David put him down."

"Because he didn't fancy him, or because he doesn't fancy men in general?"

"Because he's totally heterosexual, which also helped to make it less bitter for Edward."

"So that he wouldn't have been bitter enough to kill him? To be pretending to be outraged now about his murder?"

Philip Morgan stared at Anita, than burst out laughing. "Heavens, no! That's absurd."

"All the same, someone may mention it to the police."

"No. We're a loyal community. And we know Edward's affection for David is genuine."

Anita shrugged, and Phyllida welcomed the gap in Philip Morgan's sophistication. "So he's just trying to ease his grief by carrying a posthumous torch?"

"I'd say something like that."

"I think so far as I'm concerned there could have been an extra thing. He'd noticed me speaking to David the day before he died and I think he wanted to know what was said. David was offering to photostat the catalogues of the two Sandys exhibitions for me, which I told him."

"Poor old Edward trying to pick up crumbs. Yes, I think he would."

"So David Lester kept his affection. That was quite an achievement."

"That was David. He was a peacemaker. We'll miss him, he was one of the good ones."

"But it looks as if he masterminded a fraud."

Philip shook his head, then drained his glass and ordered second drinks. "I can't believe it, myself. Not of David."

"Of whom, then?"

He shook his head again, looking genuinely bewildered. "I don't know. I've no idea. I can't believe it's anyone on the Gallery staff. And why should it be? There could be other reasons why David was killed, reasons that have nothing at all to do with his work at the Gallery."

"I suppose so." Phyllida cast a wistful glance at the comfortable theory, which the anonymous letters made it impossible to embrace. Unless someone wanted David's death to look like it was connected with his work. And the young man in police custody was apparently separating the two crimes. . . .

"Cheers!"

Her second dry martini was in front of her. "Your good health, Philip. Mr Brooke had something else to say to me. Just as he was leaving. A warning."

"A warning?"

She thought the wariness was back. "Yes. He warned me you're a violent man, and probably unscrupulous with it." Phyllida spoke with reluctance. In her own persona she was a peacemaker too, and now she found herself struggling with a new and uncomfortable hostility towards an Anita sowing seeds of discord in a close-knit community with apparent insouciance. But the demands of her job were paramount, particularly when they were in the interests of a murder inquiry, and the murder itself ensured that the community of the Snaith Gallery staff could not survive in its old form.

"The pathetic old fool!" It seemed to be contempt rather than anger, to Phyllida's interest and relief.

"I'm glad you're taking it so well. Did you use his mug once in the tea room?"

"I repulsed him once in the gents. Not so kindly as David, but it was a shock and it disgusted me. All this fleshless parchment cover, just too too spiritual, and then . . . I'll leave it there, if you don't mind."

"I don't. So that's why Mr Brooke thinks you're violent. Unscrupulous?"

"Do we have to go on with this? I pushed him away from me and he fell. He cut his temple and there was blood but it wasn't serious. When I saw he was OK I left. It was a straightforward sex approach, by the way, not like with David. He didn't like me, and I suppose he felt humiliated, being rejected by someone he didn't like. Hence I'm violent and unscrupulous. All right?"

147

"Yes, of course. I'm not suggesting—"

"I'm sorry!" Philip Morgan was suddenly smiling. "It's not worth getting steamed up about, although I think it's a bit of a nerve. Character assassination because a bloke doesn't fancy you. If Brooke'd had murder on his mind he'd have chosen me as his victim rather than David."

"Don't think about it. Don't let it affect your day-to-day dealings with Mr Brooke, just feel superior when you have to speak to him." Phyllida realised with a frisson that her second career was demanding of her something more than she had ever needed on stage: presenting characters in her own words was turning out to be a combination of author's and actor's role, which involved creating them first with no help from a playwright. And when their motivations were alien to her, she found she was riding it on a queasy mingling of excitement and distaste. "I didn't want to cause trouble, Philip, I just wanted to know why he said what he did."

"Fair enough. In fact, you've caused encouragement." She had to lower her eyes before the challenge in his. "Shall we eat?"

The ordering of wine and food was a welcome distraction, and Phyllida was pleased to be able to approve Philip's choice of setting – unobtrusively pleasing decor, smallness and intimacy retaining enough space to feel private – in her own persona as well as Anita's.

"Philip," she said, when she had also honestly praised her smoked trout, "I think it's time I learned some facts about Frederick Sandys and his works."

She wanted them, but it was also a test, and Philip Morgan didn't pass it: the expectancy in his eyes faded to resignation via a flash of anger. *He's a violent man, Mrs Sunbury* . . . She wasn't going to be able to forget Edward Brooke's words, or the way he had said them.

"Okay. What d'you want to know?"

"It's crazy, but I don't even know what the pictures

look like. Obviously their titles have given me images of changing landscapes, but that doesn't have to be right."

"It isn't. Sandys painted in human metaphors. By which I mean *Autumn* isn't trees with falling leaves, it's a veteran of the Crimean War reclining on a bank of the Wensum with Bishop's Bridge and the unrestored Norwich Castle in the usual photographically clear Pre-Raphaelite background. They got this effect by reviving the art of fresco – painting on a wet grey-white ground like the original PRs. The old soldier's being stared at rather suspiciously by a young woman and a hefty infant on the grass beside him, but he's so busy contemplating the far side of the river he hardly seems aware of them."

"For one whose speciality the Pre-Raphaelites are not you've made a close study of the pictures." Phyllida softened the accusation with an Anita smile; she had to guard against being seen to be probing for guilt in every action and reaction of the Snaith Gallery staff.

"Yes," Philip agreed undefensively. "I don't get all that good an aesthetic buzz from them, but I find the painters interesting as a group of people, with all their well-documented Victorian ideals."

"*Spring?*"

"*Spring* is five children grouped on a woodland floor, half under a tree in full leaf – which goes to show that Sandys saw the children rather than the flora as illustrating his title. The pen and ink sketch has been around since it was drawn in 1860, and the picture's faithful to all its considerable detail and absolutely in the style of *Autumn*."

"So you think it can withstand the scandal of *Winter?*"

"I hope so." His eyes met hers frankly. "I feel it's right. *Summer*, too."

"The way you felt about *Winter?*"

149

Philip Morgan shrugged. "Yep. I felt *Winter* was right. Like the rest of us."

"*Summer*?"

"*Summer*'s a woman leaning on a wide terrace wall playing with a cat. Mature but still young."

"The Blessèd Damozel come of age?"

"You could say that, she's got all the necessary hair. David's always saying – was always saying – how good Sandys is with hair. But it's dark and controlled in the *Summer* woman and the facial features aren't so prominent as they always are with Rossetti types. David thought Sandys could have used the model he used for *The King's Daughter* which he painted in the late 1850s. This one's fashionable, by the way: 1870s waist and bustle."

"Summer landscape?"

"Just about. Like *Autumn* the season's a bit vague, even though the detail's sharp. Norwich Castle again, with the bridge over the Wensum from a different angle, and farther off. There tends to be a lack of depth in the background of Sandys' paintings, and it's here too."

"*Winter*?"

"*Winter*'s a deathbed." Philip gave the description emphasis. In an attempt, Phyllida suspected, to ease his professional embarrassment. "Two women in agonised profile from an earlier painting are almost exactly reproduced. You all right?"

"Yes, fine. Just a goose over my grave. Carry on."

"In *Tears, Idle Tears* they're bare-shouldered with classical hairstyles. Here they're country-style late Victorian, but its obvious they were modelled on the earlier figures."

"And obvious now why. It made things easier."

"I suppose so. The woman on the bed's elderly but not a crone, and there's a farmer-type with bowed head at the foot and two children, one hiding its face. Will that do?"

"Yes. Thank you. I felt it was time I knew more precisely what's been dominating the lives of my colleagues for the past half year."

"Of course. And I've told you. So could we now talk about something else? You, for instance?"

"Philip, I have to tell you—"

"What?" he interrupted angrily. She'd done well to get them half way through the meal without confrontation, and then to dent his confidence in the moment of being forced to listen to what he really wanted to say, but for the first time she could remember, Phyllida found herself more pained than pleased by the successful exercise of her talents. "D'you want to tell me you didn't feel what I felt the first time we saw one another?"

"I want to tell you," Anita said gently, "that I'm not ready to feel anything – in that way – and won't be for quite some time."

"You know well enough which way it was, though?"

"I do. And don't bully me."

"I'm sorry," he said yet again, and his smile turned her heart over. "I don't think I'm unscrupulous but I know I'm impatient. And I can't believe . . . I'm not bullying you, Anita, by asking you to tell me why you're not ready."

"Of course not, and I half knew that tonight I'd have to tell you." She drank some wine. "Philip . . . I'm here in England living at a temporary address and taking a temporary job because three months ago, what I thought and hoped was my permanent life, came to an end with the death of my husband. I found part of me had died with him, and for three months now I've been living off the top of my head and my reflexes." Phyllida wondered what it would be like to feel that way about another human being, and tried to subdue her distaste for pretending to feel it. "Everything's happening at a remove, if you can understand me. Yes, you and I had an immediate rapport,

I was aware of it, but it was miles away. And I don't know at the moment when – or if – it'll come closer. And don't tell me I've led you on because I know I haven't, the most I've done is let you see I'm at home with you."

"Yes," he said humbly. "That's the most you've done. The rest I've done myself."

He looked so defeated she risked a hand over his where it lay on the edge of the table. "Accept if you can for the moment," she said softly, "that you may have shown me that what I thought was death is only sleep, but that I'm not ready for prince charming. If you *can* accept it I'll feel a whole lot happier with you, which has to be a good thing for both of us. All right?" Phyllida pressed the unresponsive hand and withdrew her own, trying to disregard its tingling and to prevent the sensation from travelling to other parts of her body.

"I suppose so," Philip Morgan said sulkily. But when he looked up at her he smiled. "We'll see each other, then." It was something between a question and a statement.

"Sure, honey." Until Anita Sunbury disappeared into the blue, which could happen in a day, a week, a month. Certainly Phyllida's second career would always ensure there were no loose personal ends. "I like your company." This time she held her hand out and he gripped it before placing it on the table beside her glass.

"Good," he said. "So it will be as you wish, Sleeping Beauty."

"Thank you." It was time to pick up her brief. "The Director told me this afternoon, by the way, what he told you all this morning. Everyone in the Gallery must feel better, knowing the police have a suspect."

"Who's confessed to the forgeries."

"So you think the murderer could still be around?"

"I don't know. I only know I'll never believe David Lester was a cheat and a liar."

"I haven't met anyone yet who does. But somebody . . . Who would you go for in the gallery?"

"Is that fair?"

"No. I'm just interested in human nature."

To her relief he returned her smile. "It would have to be La Bennett. She told me severely this afternoon that whoever had perpetrated the fraud deserved to be punished."

"And whoever killed David Lester?"

"She didn't mention the murder. Perhaps offending against the sacred canons of art is her ultimate crime. I said, 'Punished by the *death penalty*, Pamela?', and she just about managed to blush and say of course not."

"But she could have believed David was guilty." Phyllida had a sudden memory of them face to face, David shrinking away as Miss Bennett spoke. *When do we expect the verdict? You've been very fortunate.* . . .

"I don't know. And I can't really see anyone in the Gallery committing murder, not even Pam. Carrington's *sans peur et sans reproche*, Thelma cares for nothing beyond the Gallery and its Director, you know what I think re Brooke, Deborah's a young girl who needs spending money and might as well be here as there, and I'm neither violent nor unscrupulous enough to commit murder. Shall we leave it there?"

"Of course." She would have to.

It was easy and companionable for the rest of the meal, and would have been easy and companionable on the steps of the Golden Lion – where Phyllida came to a determined halt and turned to say goodnight – if there had been no instinct in her to transform what she almost believed had been honestly offered as an affectionate kiss into a kiss of a different kind. She managed to frustrate her instinct quite quickly, but not quickly enough to prevent Philip's instant awareness and response.

When she had pulled away he held her hard by her shoulders at arm's length and stared at her. "The princess is stirring in her sleep," he said at last.

"Perhaps." There were lights across the square. "Goodnight, Philip. And thank you."

"Goodnight, princess."

His eyes on her back as she went into the hotel were as tactile as his hands and his mouth. When Phyllida got upstairs she flung herself on the bed and beat at it with her fists until her frustration and regret escaped in a fit of hysterical laughter.

Barney Barnes was about to go to bed: he'd opened the small door in the side of his office which led to what, when in conversation with his clients, he called his flat. He always spoke of it in a way to make them imagine it to be elsewhere, beyond the sleazy edge of the town where his office was the floor above a betting shop. Even if they asked to use his facilities he could let them through the door without fear of being rumbled, because the slit that held his narrow bed, hanging space and chest of drawers in tight embrace was separate from the tiny room which just managed to accommodate his lavatory, shower and wash basin.

It was quite a luxury, Barney reflected as he pulled off the tie the knot of which was already half way down his chest, to have a night without night work. It seemed a long time since he'd managed to call it a day at eleven-thirty. Because he knew he was going to be able to indulge it, he decided he felt very tired. Too tired, even, to try to get on to the client whose case had brought him within sniffing distance of a really good murder. He'd pour himself a couple of slugs of Scotch, then he'd take it through the door with him – and bugger the telephone. . . .

Its shrill ring was a two-finger response which made him jump. Then groan. He'd heard the bloody thing, and business wasn't all that brisk that he could afford to ignore it when he was actually hearing it ringing. And someone wanting him at eleven-thirty at night must want him pretty badly. . . .

Groaning again, Barney picked up the receiver.

"Barney Barnes private investigator . . . Yeah, yeah. In person. . . . Yes, of course, I want to see you, too, there are things to talk about. . . ." Barney had come slightly to attention in the chair where he was sprawling. "Sorry, I've been on an out of town job, just got back tonight. . . . You're that near, are you? All right, I was just off home, but I'll hang on. The downstairs door's not locked. . . . Fine. See you."

Barney guaranteed, when first interviewing a client, never to mention his or her name on the telephone, and it was a precaution that had become second nature. Groaning for the third time, but now with excitement, he fetched out his bottle of Scotch and a couple of glasses – this was a case where it could pay to appear generous – immediately pouring into one of them and taking a deep drink.

He heard the door below as he was taking another one, his client had been very close by. He got up and unlocked his glass door as the familiar shadow appeared on it.

"Come in, come in. You're lucky to find me here, it's not often I'm off the job so early." He didn't mention clients' names face to face with them in his office, either. Just in case during one of his many absences someone had managed to get past his flimsy security and plant a bug. . . . "You'll have a drink?"

"Thank you, no. I've been out to dinner and I've had quite enough for someone in charge of a car."

"At least sit down while we're talking."

"Thank you. I'm sorry to be bothering you so late,

Barney, but in view of the news you'll hardly be surprised."

"Well, no. . . ." Barney ventured a knowing smile. There could be profit of a different kind to be made on this particular case.

"I'm afraid I haven't got your reports with me – I wouldn't leave them in the car and I haven't had the sort of evening where I could carry them around. So could you get the file out, there's one particular point. . . ."

"Sure." Barney got up from behind his desk and went over to the battered green filing cabinet that stood in the angle of the window and the wall facing his inner door. This meant that while he was rummaging in its top drawer his back was to his client and his arms were up as if he was reacting to a threat from a gun.

But it wasn't a gun which turned Barney's grasp of the folder he was seeking into the last action of his life. It was a knife, which his client inserted in one strong movement into the point on Barney's back which led most directly to his heart.

The client had Barney by the shoulders before he could fall backwards, and so was able to guide him on to his stomach and then pull the knife out as smoothly as it had been pushed in, before transferring the folder to a briefcase and then carrying out a leisurely and thorough turnover – first of the office and then of the flat, where a snort of laughter was involuntary – the reaction Barney had always been afraid of.

Chapter Twelve

"I was getting a bit over-confident." Peter began speaking hurriedly the moment Phyllida entered his office. "I was beginning to think my private relationship – or should I call it yours? – with Detective Chief Superintendent Kendrick meant I'd no further need of the services of my tame DS. But he was in touch earlier to let me know that I have."

He wasn't meeting her eyes. "You saw me just now outside the Golden Lion?" she ask

"Well, yes. Not as a Peeping Tom, I was just thinking you might be back and about to come across – sorry about the pun – and there you were putting on a splendid performance."

"It's under control, the fictions worked a dream." Phyllida smiled reassuringly, caught Peter's eye, and held it firmly until she was sure he was over his embarrassment. "Philip wants more than Anita can give him at the moment, but he's content to wait as a friend. That was a friendly salute, Peter." She regained his eyes, not minding in the least that he had witnessed their kiss.

"Of course," he agreed. "It's just that you're such a good actress. You'll have a Scotch?"

"Please. What service did your tame DS offer you this time? And why, seeing you're now in cahoots with the man at the top?"

"Well, you know what I think. . . ." Restored to his

usual mode of animated relaxation, Peter busied himself at his drinks cabinet. "I think he's feeling left out of things, as if our special relationship's been taken over, so when he had a chance to tell me something before Kendrick does – and we're both realistic enough to know Kendrick mayn't, of course – he took it. Cheers!" Peter took a gulp of his drink, his eyes sparkling. "Phyllida, the chap helping the police with their inquiries claims to have spent the night Lester was murdered in a flat on Seaminster promenade belonging to the Director of the Snaith Gallery."

"Charles Carrington? You're joking."

"I haven't finished. The flat in question was rented by David Lester in the summer for his sister's family. Since then it's been on a long lease in a name which has turned out to have an accommodation address. The chap told the police the man who called himself Lester sent him the key to the flat ages ago so that he could deliver the three pictures there, then rang him recently and told him to spend Wednesday night at the flat, giving the impression he'd be going too and they'd meet at last. The chap insists there was bed linen, breakfast food and so on, but no one came and he left as instructed in the early morning and went back to London."

"Has anyone been living in the flat during the current lease?"

"That's one of the difficulties: the flats are let furnished and equipped with household necessaries, so it's hard to know whether or not anyone's actually living there. The police are certain someone's been going in to clean but there weren't any signs of recent occupation, no bed made up or any perishable food about, which makes the unfortunate artist's claim to have slept there and eaten breakfast even flimsier than it was to start with. It's got me thinking about the Wallace case in Liverpool in the 'thirties. An insurance agent – I think he was an insurance agent, I'm not as good on fact as I am on fiction – received a telephone call one evening telling him there was some business for him in a suburb the other side of the city from where he lived. So he went off leaving his wife at home, in search of an address that turned out not to exist, and when he got home his wife had been murdered."

"What happened to him?"

"He swore he was innocent, but he was convicted of murder. He wasn't executed, and eventually he was released and I think died soon after. And then it was discovered a few years ago that a younger man was the most likely murderer."

"And had set Wallace up?"

"Yes. So I'm wondering if someone set the artist up, his alibi's just as absurd. He's proclaiming himself guilty of fraud, by the way. I gather he's proud of it and now he's been rumbled he's insisting he painted all three pictures."

"As the Chief Super was kind enough to tell Mrs Cookson this morning," Phyllida said "Charles Carrington and Philip Morgan insist that *Spring* and *Summer* are the real thing. Whether they are or not, I was hardly surprised when Mr Carrington told Anita this afternoon that the police haven't found any evidence their suspect painted any of the pictures – if he was going to earn his money he was going to do exactly as he was told, and his control would have told him to destroy the evidence. . . . Peter, d'you think perhaps there wasn't a control, that this young man thought it all up by himself?"

"So why was David Lester murdered?"

"Because of knowing enough about Sandys to make the forger/murderer afraid of him?"

"But Lester appeared to believe from the start that the pictures were genuine."

"Yes, and there are the anonymous letters. I'm only

thinking aloud. There are so many possibilities I just can't help trying out theories all the time."

"But what look like the facts point to there being only one possibility," Peter said. He flopped back in his chair and put his fingertips together, his habitual indication that he was thinking deeply. "David Lester inaugurated the fraud, and when he made it plain to the man who carried it out that there was to be no more business, that man decided he'd be safer with Lester dead. And turned Lester's house over to make sure there was nothing there to connect them."

"While knowing there could be something in Lester's office files."

"There was. My tame DS also told me that was how the police got on to the fellow."

"There you are, then. You can see what I mean?"

"Oh, yes. I've been theorising, too. If Lester isn't the master forger it could be he knew who is and was killed so he couldn't shop him. But that theory doesn't fit too well with the anonymous letters, unless the master forger was trying to make Lester appear to be the guilty one. The other idea I came up with is – no, I'm getting silly."

"Me too. Although my head tells me a lot of the pro-David Lester reaction could be the guilt syndrome that you mustn't speak ill of the dead and it would be sacrilegious to accuse anyone who's been murdered of having committed a fraud, at the same time my instincts want me to stick my neck out and say I can't see the man Mrs Cookson met abusing his talents. That's silly enough, isn't it – you can hardly lay claim to a gut feeling that someone's incapable of forgery. And I keep thinking about the profile and wondering if and how it fits in. Oh, and by the way," Phyllida hastened on, under Peter's jocularly disapproving eye, "Anita's been invited to join the rest of the staff for Sunday lunch buffet-style at the Carringtons this weekend. Apparently they were so confident about *Winter* they'd arranged the lunch in celebration of the recovery of three lost Sandys. They were going to cancel it, and then they decided it might be helpful to get together quietly, away from the Gallery."

"A wake rather than a party. Wakes can be cheering affairs, though, and draw a line under unhappy events. Only they'll have to go through it all again when Lester's body's released."

"I suppose so. Oh, Peter, I feel so sorry for everybody. I don't know if it's because my contacts in this second career of mine are all make-believe, but I'm finding it so uncomfortably easy to feel unhappy about other people's tragedies. As if when I take on a character I have to accord it a part of my mind as well as my appearance and behaviour." Phyllida gave an involuntary shudder.

"I don't think it's that," Peter pronounced judicially. "I don't think either Mrs Sunbury or Mrs Cookson has it in her to be upset at what's happened anything like as much as Phyllida Moon has."

"Thanks. I hope you're right." He was certainly right so far as Philip Morgan was concerned. "Anyway, at least I can assure you that wherever my compassion has its origin, it won't interfere with my work."

"I know."

Phyllida wondered if behind his encouraging smile Peter was thinking of Philip Morgan, too. "And I know your professionalism will enable you to see how brilliantly beneficial to David Lester the fraud would have been if his 'instrument' hadn't turned on him. He'd earned fat commissions on the first two pictures, and unless he'd sent his forger anachronistic materials for *Winter* by mistake, which is hardly credible, when it was declared a fake he'd have pointed the police at him some way or other and then denied what would look like his ridiculous accusations about 'Lester' and the flats."

"I agree the forger could have got hold of the Lester

part easily enough, with David's name being associated with the Sandys in the Press, but the flat's another thing. How could Lester have explained away his claim about that?"

"There you have me. So I fall back on the suggestion that David Lester masterminded *Spring* and *Summer* and left it there, having rewarded his artist into what he hoped was obscurity, and the forger decided to go ahead on his own with *Winter* and wasn't as lucky with his supplier as he'd been with the first two pictures. He could have sent the anonymous letters as a sort of revenge on Lester for refusing to sponsor him for *Winter*. Receiving them, and *Winter* turning up as much out of the blue for him as for everyone else, would explain Lester's acute anxiety. . . . We're getting ourselves into an awful muddle," Peter went on, shaking his head after a few minutes' silence in which they stared hopefully at one another. "Let's have another drink. And let's stop speculating," he suggested, when he had poured them. "It isn't going to get us anywhere, is it?"

"No. And I'm starting to wonder if Anita at the Snaith Gallery is going to get us anywhere either."

"It might get us some more careful confidences from Detective Chief Superintendent Kendrick. If you can bear it, I think you should stay there until there's an arrest, or he relegates the case to the back burner."

"Or it's still on the front page in April when I have to answer the call of my first career. . . . Peter, what an appalling thought! The Snaith Gallery's a nice enough place, but I want to do a few other jobs for you before I have to break off."

"I'll be surprised if it's on the front page next week. It's cut and dried, Phyllida. I'm sorry, but it has to be."

"I suppose so." She was shocked by the strength of her sense of defeat. "Anyway, it's Saturday tomorrow and tonight I'm going home."

*   *   *

162

Paul Fisher's voice was beginning to get on Kendrick's nerves. It was managing to maintain its mid-Atlantic neutrality, revealing its origins only in the occasional prominent glottal stop or diphthong, but its light, reedy quality seemed to grow steadily more penetrating as the man became more seriously self-concerned.

"Tell us about yourself, Mr Fisher," Kendrick invited, half an hour into the unproductive Saturday morning session, for what he hoped might prove a useful respite as well as temporarily removing the self-pity from Fisher's voice.

Fisher turned to Felicity McKay, the attractive young duty solicitor sitting alongside him. "Go ahead," she said, looking with raised eyebrows at the policemen.

Fisher shrugged. "Two parents, I was lucky. One brother who works in a bank and so far as I know isn't on the fiddle." Kendrick had been right, the voice was instantly less irritating, and he had already learned something from his diversion: his man had a sense of humour. The discovery so far on in their dialogue brought an unexpected sense of regret that he'd been responsible for suppressing it from the moment he'd held his ID up in Fisher's doorway. "I wasn't much good at school, but I always knew I could paint. Perhaps that was what kept me out of trouble, Mr Kendrick, there was plenty of it going, in and around Acacia Terrace, if I'd wanted it. But I kept my nose clean, I mean I kept paint on the end of it, and I got to Goldsmith's. Oh, God. . . ." Fisher's thin, pert face crumpled, and he dropped his head to the table in front of him.

"All right, Mr Fisher, there's no need for that." Kendrick spoke gruffly, to hide his sudden unwelcome impulse of sympathy. "Come along, now. You did very well to get yourself such good training. it's just a pity the way you've used it, if you're telling us the truth."

"I painted those three pictures!" Fisher's head came

up as he glared at Kendrick, and his body stiffened. He was proud of the lesser crime.

"There's one aspect of this business we haven't been into yet," DS Wetherhead intervened. "Why did you send David Lester two anonymous letters?"

Kendrick would have sworn the astonishment was genuine. But if Fisher was guilty of murder and forgery he'd have the skill and nerve to fake it.

"Anonymous letters? I don't know anything about any anonymous letters!"

"David Lester received them within a couple of weeks of each other while the Snaith Gallery was awaiting the verdict on *Winter*. They both foretold it would be proved a forgery, and that Mr Lester would suffer when this came to light."

"So I forged a picture, then wrote anonymous letters saying it was a forgery? You have to be joking." Fisher remembered his brief, and turned to her. "It's crazy," he said.

"If anonymous letters were received," she told him gently, "the police have to ask you about them."

"Thank you," Kendrick said. "So tell me, Mr Fisher."

Paul Fisher leaned across the table and held out his hands. "You've got to believe me," he said. "I haven't killed anyone. I couldn't. I can only just kill flies. Oh God," he said turning to Ms McKay. "How can I make them believe me?"

"By continuing to tell the truth."

"Oh, I'll do that. I've done it and I'll go on doing it. I painted the three pictures, but I didn't kill the man who gave me the commission. That's the truth, Mr Kendrick."

"Had Mr Lester offered you any more work?" Kendrick inquired, trying to disregard the impact on him of Fisher's plea.

164

"No."

"But you'd have liked some?"

"Who wouldn't, with skills like mine?"

"Quite. So you felt frustrated, and you asked him for more?"

"Yes, I did."

"And when he still said there wouldn't be any you thought you'd go round to his house and try to persuade him to change his mind."

"I've told you, I didn't know where he lived! I don't know now, with not being allowed to see or hear any news. Put me on the rack, pull my toenails out, I still won't tell you Lester's address because I don't know it!"

"You can tell me his telephone number, though."

"No!" Fisher turned his anguished gaze on Miss McKay, who nodded encouragingly. "I never rang him, he always rang me! Always said at the end of a call when he'd call again, and always did. He never gave me a number any more than he gave me an address!"

"This line of questioning is producing only distress for my client," Ms KcKay observed.

"And you won't find any evidence in his house that I was there because I never was!" Fisher said.

"We won't find any evidence of your presence in David Lester's house because you made sure there wouldn't be by turning it over," DS Wetherhead amended, and Fisher groaned and covered his face with his hands.

"I suggest you leave things there for the moment," Ms McKay said. "It's obvious my client is becoming unacceptably distressed."

"Like I said, I've never been to Lester's place, I don't know where he lived," Fisher repeated desperately, as he raised his head. Kendrick watched the blotched pink imprint of his fingers die slowly out of his pale cheeks. "But if I did, and if I'd been there . . . what would have been the point in turning his house over when I knew there was no way I could turn over his office files?"

"The point would have been that you could make the point you're making now," DS Wetherhead said, and Ms McKay clicked her tongue.

"Oh, God," Fisher said, and Kendrick concluded the interview verbally and then leaned over to switch the machine off.

"I'll see you both later," he promised.

"Don't forget your time's running out," Ms McKay reminded him.

"I know our time's running out," Kendrick said angrily, as he strode towards his office. "Come with me, Fred, for heaven's sake, I want to think aloud to you."

DS Clarkson was leaning against Kendrick's door when Kendrick charged round the corner, and stumbled slightly in his eagerness to be seen to be standing on his own two feet. But he continued to smile.

"What's the joke, Jim?" Kendrick asked tartly.

"Good news, sir. We've just heard that Fisher's fingerprint – a beaut, by all accounts – has been found on the back of the canvas of *Winter*."

"Thank you, Jim." Kendrick met grin with grin, and turned to include DS Wetherhead. "Good news, indeed. Perhaps you'd be kind enough to take Ms McKay aside if she hasn't left the building, inform her of this development, and suggest she hangs on to support her client when he's charged with forgery."

"I'd be delighted, sir." DS Clarkson spoke with enthusiasm: it wasn't often a junior detective found him or herself in the position of proffering bad news to the cunningly competent Felicity McKay.

"Good lad." Kendrick went into his office and sat down, motioning Fred Wetherhead to the other comfortable seat and all at once feeling flat and drained. He'd known about *Winter*, known Fisher was speaking the truth when he claimed to have painted it, he hadn't learned anything . . . But he'd gained the right to question Fisher about the murder of David Lester without looking at the clock. He should be happy, for God's sake.

"Good, eh, sir?"

"Very good, Fred. Good enough to be the first piece of circumstantial evidence that's come our way for either crime."

"Only second best to finding a Fisher fingerprint at The Cedars. And they're still looking."

"Yes. . . ."

"All right, sir?"

"As right as can be expected, Fred!" Kendrick snapped. He sometimes wished his DS wasn't so confoundedly aware of him all the time, even though he knew it stemmed from admiration and affection. And he was annoyed that his moment of weakness had showed in his face. The weakness of acknowledging that he would have been dismayed rather than triumphant if Fisher's dabs had been found in Lester's house, because of his instincts telling him the young man wasn't a killer. . . . "Sorry, Fred." Kendrick brought his strong will to bear on himself and smiled genially at his DS. "It's just frustration."

"That's all right, sir, I can understand how you must feel. I've just been thinking . . . I know it's all right for the time being, we can hold Fisher on the evidence of *Winter*. But will we be getting on to the buyers of the other two pictures and asking if we can take them to pieces?"

"Oh, God." Kendrick gave a heavy sigh. "I suppose so, in due course. I'm always glad to spare the innocent where I can, but the main reason I've kept Carrington's secret so far is because I didn't want to muddy the murder waters. Now we've got evidence to charge Fisher with fraud I'm afraid we're going to have to be exhaustive

167

over the lesser crime because of its being the bird in hand. We'll call on Carrington in the morning and break the bad news. No need to wait for the morning to charge Lester." Kendrick got wearily to his feet and forced himself to speak with enthusiasm. "Come along, Fred, let's pay a visit to the duty sergeant."

Chapter Thirteen

Barney Barnes's body was discovered early on Saturday afternoon, by a would-be female client who went screaming down the street.

Kendrick's annoyance at being disturbed during another fruitless session with Paul Fisher evaporated with the word *murder*, and when he learned that the murder victim was a private eye, he told his uniformed informant he would be in Barney's office as quickly as it took to get there. When he got back to his own office, Kendrick rang Peter Piper Private Investigator, wishing it was a weekday, but to his pleased surprise Dr Piper answered in person. Kendrick asked if he would do him the favour of dropping in there and then for a chat. Peter said truthfully that he would be only too delighted.

"Know anything about the Ancaster Detective Agency? Bartholomew Barnes?" Kendrick inquired, when the tea tray he had managed to rustle up had been deposited.

"Barney Barnes? He's an old hand and a loner. Divorced years ago, no visible girlfriend. He's never even had an assistant, as far as I know. Does his own typing and accounting as well as sleuthing." Peter had sometimes thought, with a twinge of unrealistic regret, that Barney Barnes, with his unshaven chin and rusting cabinets, was closer to his own cherished image of a Chandler hero than he himself would ever be.

"Unlike you, Dr Piper. How many people do you

employ?" Kendrick found himself asking in a casual conversational tone.

"Three," Peter answered promptly. "Secretary-cum-bookkeeper, and two field assistants."

"One of them being Miss Bowden."

"That's right." Peter grinned at the flash of disbelief across the Chief Super's eyes as if he didn't see it. "I don't really know Barney, Mr Kendrick, we just have a drink at the odd Association of British Investigators jamboree, and as the only two PIs in Seaminster we've occasionally traded information. Can I ask why you're interested?"

"Surely. And you'll know anyway tonight when you turn on your TV. He's just been found murdered. Lying on his office floor with a knife wound in his heart."

"Poor old Barney." Peter's breath came fast for a few minutes, he was doubly shocked. For Barney, and because it might have been himself. "He did tend to take on some gritty stuff. Stuff I might have thought twice about." *If I'd been offered it*, Peter added wistfully in his head, with another spurt of unrealistic regret. Barney would surely have thought twice about taking on the requests to find missing pets which reached the Peter Piper Agency on a monthly average. . . . "Did you yourself see—"

"Yes. I've just got back. His office had been turned over. Perhaps I'm being fanciful, Dr Piper, wanting to find a connection, but it seemed to me that whoever went through Mr Barnes's effects approached the job in very much the same way as whoever went through David Lester's."

"You mean – the degree of chaos?"

"I don't know what I mean," Kendrick confessed. "But that could be part of it."

"It couldn't have been your art forger, unless Barney's been dead for a day or two, in which case he'd have to have fallen on very hard times to have had no visitors."

"He died last night round about eleven, twelve."

"Forced entry?"

"No. The doors upstairs and down were unlocked and there was a bottle of Scotch on the desk with two glasses. One had whisky in it and the other was dry, but Barney could have been despatched before he got round to wetting it. When did you last see him, Dr Piper? It could be wonderfully helpful if you saw him yesterday."

Peter shook his head, laughing to hide his shock. "I'm afraid not, Chief Superintendent, it was yonks ago. But if you want an alibi I can easily—"

Kendrick shook his head in turn, not showing he had been looking for the assurance Piper had virtually given him that he hadn't seen Bartholomew Barnes the night before. "No, no, I was just hoping for a bit of help. We'll go through all his case files, of course, but it's unlikely a significant one will still be among them. Did you ever see his domestic arrangements?"

"No." Peter's expression posed a query. "I've never been to his home and I've only been in his office once. I thought you said that's where he died."

"It is. And he lived the other side of a door, in it. Bedroom, bathroom, kitchen, in miniature. All gone through as well. It was the way the kitchen was tackled that first made me think of David Lester."

"Poor old Barney." Peter had a sudden vivid memory of the man leaning on a bar counter somewhere, his breath a bit gamey as he said how good it was to get away from the office. "He always talked as though he lived away from his work, in a better part of town. But I expect it suited him to be on the spot. I find I spend a lot of my own time in my office, although I do live elsewhere, Mr Kendrick."

"Ex-directory." Kendrick had tried to look it up.

"In self defence against the anguished ladies who lose their Smutties and their Tiddles. Oh, Lord, I could have put that a better way, couldn't I?"

Both men experienced the refreshment of momentarily uncontrollable laughter, but when Dr Piper had left Kendrick sat on behind his desk, growing increasingly uneasy that his irrational gut feeling that Fisher was innocent was acquiring some substance. But fanciful was the word he had used to Piper, and fanciful it had to be, to see a connection between two goings over. There was no reason whatsoever to connect Barney Barnes's death with David Lester's.

Sometime during a Saturday of housework, gardening, completing a chapter of her ongoing history of women and the stage, and absorbing Peter's news of the murder of Seaminster's other PI, Phyllida reluctantly decided it was time she started trying to play herself as whole-heartedly as she played her other characters. But she awoke on Sunday morning already looking forward to a respite from the effort, and was glad to drive to the Golden Lion and assume Anita.

And receive the telephone call she had half expected from Philip Morgan, suggesting he call for her.

He arrived smiling and apparently relaxed.

"You look wonderful," he said without overtones, as he helped her into the car.

"Thank you, Philip." Her weakness of Friday night had shocked her into total vigilance, and it was easy to tell him in a friendly way that it was good to see him.

"And to see you," he responded lightly.

The Carringtons lived beyond Marlborough Drive, where suburb began to give place to country, in a small stone manor house. As they rounded the one bend in the drive they saw Charles Carrington, a tall

172

slender woman close at his side, surveying some winter jasmine on the wall beside the front door, in the company of Thelma and Deborah. The visitors were still in their jackets, and had evidently just emerged from Thelma's small red Renault. Carrington was as elegant in his weekend gear of light blue pullover and cords as in his grey weekday suits, and the woman who must be his wife earned Phyllida's instant aesthetic approval with her smooth cap of shining dark gold hair and simple yellow-gold skirt and waistcoat over a gold silk blouse. When she turned round at the sound of another car, Phyllida saw sombre, classic features assume a hostessly smile.

"The perfect couple," Philip murmured. "Don't they look good?"

"Yes. And it's good it's a fine day. Going round the garden will help everyone."

Mr Carrington was opening Anita's door. "Welcome!" he said. "We're so glad you could come. This is my wife Imelda. This is Anita Sunbury, darling."

"Mrs Sunbury," Imelda Carrington repeated as Phyllida got out of the car. "Thank you for joining us today."

"It was very good of you to ask me. . . ." Phyllida wasn't revising her immediate judgment that Mrs Carrington was a beautiful woman, she was just wondering, as her hostess spoke to her and they looked into one another's eyes, what it was that was missing.

"Would you like to look round the garden?" Charles Carrington was asking. "Before you take off your coats? There isn't much to see as yet, but we inherited an old and well-designed layout and it's such a fine – ah, here comes Edward!"

Mr Brooke's shabby old Ford was moving very slowly, with Miss Bennett's equally neglected Mini about a foot from its boot. As the drive widened she passed it, drew up beside the Renault, and was out of her car while Mr Brooke was still wavering towards the other obvious space.

"Morning!" she called out as she banged the door.

"Pamela!" Charles Carrington went forward to greet her, and after a moment's pause his wife turned and walked across to where Mr Brooke was just coming to a halt.

"Hello, Edward," Phyllida heard her say. She had an attractive voice, low and soft, but whatever was missing was missing from there, too . . . Phyllida pulled herself up, while accepting that it was impossible not to be aware of Imelda Carrington. In any gathering, her beauty and distinction would be outstanding.

Anita strolled up to her. "What a lovely place this is!"

"Thank you." The smile didn't reach the large blue eyes, then or as Mrs Carrington helped Edward Brooke out of his car. "There you are, Edward," she said. "Are you coming round the garden?"

"If everyone else is," Mr Brooke responded without enthusiasm. But he was an indoor person, his milieu a book-lined room artificially lit, which was where at that moment he would much prefer to be. . . . It was disconcerting, Phyllida reflected, the way her second career had put a magnifying glass into her hand and forced her to hold it up to whoever she was observing, a magnifying glass seemingly powerful enough to let her see inside their heads. And to over-stimulate her ever-ready imagination. . . .

"I think we are all met," Charles Carrington was saying gravely. "And all very much aware that David isn't with us." He had done right to mention their loss, and following the collective sigh and murmur there was a noticeable relaxation in the tension which had seized the small group as it stood around. Only Imelda Carrington continued to stand motionless, staring ahead of her as if unaware that her husband had put his arm across her shoulder. "Before we look for consolation in the garden, I must tell you what I learned earlier this morning. What I gather is firm evidence that the man in police custody painted *Winter* has prompted the police to investigate the credentials of *Spring* and *Summer*, and they will be approaching the buyers." Mr Carrington held up his hand as Miss Bennett snorted and Thelma gave a cry of protest. "This is something the police have to do," he said, "as you'll all realise if you think about it. They have to present the pictures to experts selected by themselves. What you have to remember is that *Spring* and *Summer* have already passed their test, they'll simply be re-taking it. So there's nothing to worry about. I just thought you should know."

"Thank you, Charles," said Edward, and there was an approving murmur.

Imelda Carrington gave a noticeable shiver and her husband turned to look at her. "You're cold, darling, we must put our coats on, too. I'll get them."

"I'll get them, Charles." Mrs Carrington put her hand up to her husband's, where it lay on her shoulder, and pressed it as she turned to smile at him. Warmth came into her eyes and told Phyllida what it was that her beauty had lacked until that moment.

Soul.

Which was an absurd judgment. What soul could she see in Pamela Bennett's petulance or Edward Brooke's lack of emotion?

Phyllida gave herself a mental shaking as, with Philip at her side, she followed the Carringtons through a stone archway, and turned her attention firmly to the beauty of their garden.

Imelda Carrington took no part in her husband's commentary, which lasted an interesting half hour and brought the party back to the house chilly but soothed.

As they were straggling towards the door of the lushly-planted conservatory a bell on the corner of the house wall began to jangle and Mrs Carrington walked quickly ahead and disappeared inside.

"Telephone," her husband explained as he watched her. "Shall we have our drinks in here? It's heated."

There was a ripple of intrigued assent. "It's just like Kew Gardens!" Deborah exclaimed.

Phyllida could see what she meant. The central palm was as high as the dome, and the aesthetically angled seats were framed in varied exotica.

"If you'd like to give me your coats I'll take them inside – Ah!" Charles Carrington came to attention as his wife appeared in the doorway to the house. "Am I wanted, darling?"

"You're all wanted." Imelda Carrington was smiling, but there remained that curious blankness in her beautiful eyes and Phyllida saw the stretch of her mouth as an act of will. "That was Sonia Harding's husband. About an hour ago she became the mother of a son."

Phyllida wondered if that was Imelda's trouble. Childlessness, or the loss of children. No one had mentioned junior Carringtons in Mrs Sunbury's hearing.

Thelma gave a shriek of delight and rushed for the house. Imelda held out a restraining hand, renewing her smile and tingeing it with warmth. "He's rung off, I'm afraid, I think he wanted to make some more calls. Mother and baby are both doing well."

"He's early!" Thelma said excitedly. "If you hadn't appeared, Anita, he could have been born in the Gallery!"

"New life," said their host. "So it goes."

"David's life wasn't old!"

Edward Brooke's plaintive protest was a rebuke, which Charles Carrington accepted with a smile. "I know, Edward, I know. I was just commenting on

176

the cycle. As we lose we gain. Now, none of us of course has seen this gathering as a celebration, but I think David would approve of our toasting Sonia's baby in champagne."

Which he had not, of course, orginally intended offering them, but the continuing legato of his movements as he took the coats and carried them into the house told Phyllida, not to her surprise, that he maintained a supply. After another moment of blank horizon-gazing, his wife came forward and suggested everyone found a seat. "I'll bring the eaty bits out here to you."

"I'll help you, if I may." Anita strolled towards her, and with another effortful smile, Imelda nodded. In the large, elegantly furnished room beyond the door, dishes of savoury titbits had been distributed among the small tables. "I'm so sorry about what's happened," Anita said, as she picked up two of them. "I only met David Lester briefly, but he seemed like a very nice man."

"That's what my husband always said."

"You didn't know him yourself?"

Imelda straightened up, a dish in either hand, and looked at Anita empty-eyed. "Charles thinks highly of his staff and they like working for him, but we tend not to meet them out of school."

A cold fish and a snob. The definition came inevitably into Phyllida's mind, and she was surprised to find herself rejecting it as superficial and inaccurate because of an instinct that Imelda Carrington was nothing at that moment beyond a living, breathing attempt to keep some enormous emotion under control. Sorrow? Anger? Fear?

Phyllida reproved herself again. A selfish woman forced against her inclinations to entertain the staff of her husband's business turning into a soul in torment? And, Phyllida reflected, it was time she accepted that her work on this particular case had come to an unsatisfactory close and lunch with the Carringtons was simply a bonus.

"I see," Anita said. "I expect that's wise of you."

Words and tone were a reproach, but Imelda Carrington appeared unaware of it. "Thanks for your help," she said, turning to go back into the conservatory.

Phyllida followed slowly, seeing Philip awaiting Anita in the doorway. His hand on her shoulder produced an instant warmth which she tried unsuccessfully to ignore as she put one dish down on the table near Thelma and Deborah and the other in front of Edward Brooke, who, like Pamela Bennett, was sitting alone. She was starting towards Pamela when Philip seized her hand and led her to an unoccupied seat. At the same moment Imelda Carrington's vacant gaze lighted on Mr Brooke and she sat down beside him.

"How are you then, Edward?"

Not quite so formal as she had led Anita to believe, but Phyllida, despite her continuing efforts, still couldn't rid herself of the idea that all their hostess's energies were concentrated on holding herself in check.

Against what, for goodness' sake? Perhaps it was as well she was so aware of Philip beside her, diffusing by his mere presence the absurd Sherlock Holmes tendencies she was beginning to believe must go inevitably with her assumption of disguise.

"All right?" he asked softly.

"Fine."

"Good. I don't know whether I'm depressed or not."

"If you are, it's your own fault."

"Is it? I still think—"

A popping champagne cork from inside the house made Deborah cry out and Philip break off with a curse. Phyllida welcomed the diversion, and was reminded by the exaggerated reactions all round, despite the fact of David Lester having been killed with a knife not a gun, that the garden tour had been a palliative rather than a cure.

Charles Carrington had placed a tray of champagne flutes on the largest of the tables, and now appeared determinedly smiling and carrying a gently fizzing bottle which he proceeded to pour. With a quick stretch of the lips towards Edward Brooke, Imelda Carrington got to her feet and began to hand the glasses round.

"Did Sonia give him a name?" Thelma asked.

"No." Another grudging ghost of a smile.

"To Sonia's first-born, then," Charles Carrington announced. "Young Master Harding!"

The repetition was a confused murmur, some people choosing the first half of the title and some the second. "I do love champagne!" Deborah enthused, before sneezing on the bubbles.

"And to David's life," Charles continued gravely. "A double celebration, after all."

"David!"

The response this time was unanimous, and then Pamela Bennett gave a shout of pain, buried her face in her hands, and began a noisy weeping.

"Pamela!" Charles was beside her, his arm round her convulsing shoulders. His wife stood immobile, biting her lip. "My dear girl! Whatever is it?"

"It's David, of course!" Pamela dropped her hands and glared at them. With her nose red as well as shiny and her lifeless hair in wisps round her blotched face, she had plumbed new depths of unattractiveness. "It's the outrage of an innocent, brilliant life being destroyed! We should be raging at the heavens!"

"Oh, my dear, we are, we are. But it won't bring him back." Charles Carrington looked at his wife's mask of a face as he stepped away from Miss Bennett, and Phyllida thought something in it caught his attention. He murmured to her as he put his arm round her, and

179

there was another instant of affectionate response which brought her fleetingly to life.

Meanwhile, Thelma had left her seat and was squeezing in beside Pamela, smiling at her approvingly as she put her hand on her arm. Deborah looked as though she might cry as well, Edward Brooke heaved a deep sigh, and even Philip muttered, "Who'd have thought it?" under his breath. Pamela Bennett's outburst had altered her colleagues' perception of her in one dramatic moment and brought her into the category of caring human being. "You cry," Thelma advised, patting the unresponsive arm. "You've been so strong, but everyone needs to express their sorrow. You cry."

"I'm all right." Pamela gulped, then blew her nose. "Sorry about that. It's because I'm so angry."

"We all are." Thelma pushed the stem of Miss Bennett's glass between the fingers clenched on the table top. "Have a drink, Pam, it'll help."

"I don't need a drink!" But she lifted the glass and drank deep. "Whoever forged the wretched *Winter* killed David to make him look like the guilty one!" she announced angrily as she banged the glass down. Phyllida saw Charles Carrington wince.

"That would be a terrible motive for murder," Anita murmured. But Phyllida and Peter had considered it. "And you don't think he was, honey?"

"Of course he wasn't!" Passionate conviction had brought Miss Bennett to her feet. "The mere idea's disgusting. David was a true scholar! Utterly honest! I'd stake my life on it!"

"Pamela's right." Charles Carrington's voice sounded above the general consenting chatter, informing Phyllida that the Chief Superintendent's early morning revelations had not included the discovery in David Lester's office files. "Now," he went on gently, "let's think today of David the friend and colleague, and of Sonia's baby." His second sip of champagne was slow and ceremonious and even Pamela Bennett followed suit. Then she sat down, and hands began reaching out for nuts and crisps.

Charles Carrington nodded his satisfaction, and turned to where his wife had been standing. "Darling. . . ." He and Phyllida noticed on the same instant that she was missing, and Phyllida wished she could have matched her swift disappearance into the house, not least to avert further attention on the part of Philip Morgan.

"Anita . . ." He didn't appear to have moved, but his shoulder, thigh and foot were in touch with hers.

"I'll get up, Philip," Anita murmured, "if you go on ignoring what I said to you on Friday." It was a wrench to break the three contacts. "The password's patience."

"All right. I'm sorry."

"You could say we met at the wrong time." She turned away from the inevitable thought that any time would have been wrong for Phyllida Moon. "But that doesn't have to be fatal unless you insist on it."

"I won't." Philip gave an exaggerated groan, then assumed the smile he had worn when they had met that morning. "I promise."

"See that you stick to it. Ah, thank you."

Charles had returned and was refilling glasses. "Bring them in with you," he advised. "Lunch is ready."

Imelda Carrington and a small, dark-haired woman were standing beside a central glass table in a room where the contrast between an original fireplace and gracefully modern fittings reminded Phyllida of Carrington's office at the Snaith Gallery. The table was laden with cold food; Phyllida found it hard to visualise Mrs Carrington as a cook. But the dark woman, whose bustling energy as she proffered dishes was in almost comical contrast to Imelda's minimal movements, told them her employer's role had been the creative one.

"Madam just can't help being artistic. Food, flowers,

181

it's all the same." Phyllida thought she saw concern in the smile directed at their hostess. "Even when she's fighting a migraine like she was all day yesterday."

"Hush, Bea." Imelda gave a return smile that appeared to be spontaneous as well as reproachful. "I'm perfectly well now."

The little woman shrugged and indicated the table. Imelda shook her head. "There you are, you see. Not eating."

"Leave it, please," Imelda said softly.

"Migraines take her appetite away," Charles explained, putting his arm round his wife's shoulders, and she smiled up at him, life briefly in her eyes.

So that's all right, Phyllida told herself, trying to believe it. Trying to believe Imelda Carrington's sickness was of the body rather than the spirit. And not succeeding.

By the time they reached the puddings the collective consumption of champagne was threatening the gravitas of the occasion and twice Deborah received murmured reproofs from Thelma for bursting out laughing. Phyllida decided the mingling of pain and pleasure imposed by the birth of Sonia's baby made the occasion even more difficult than it would have been if mourning had been the sole order of the day.

"Ladies, upstairs!" Bea ordered, when her vigorous promotion of the food at last produced headshakes all round. "Madam's room's at the top of the stairs on the right, the door's open and her bathroom's en suite. Gentlemen to the downstairs cloakroom!"

Thelma and Deborah left the room together, and Philip squeezed Anita's elbow and followed Charles and Edward. Bea, despite Imelda's languid protests, began a brisk clearing up, and Pamela and Anita followed Imelda back to the conservatory, where Pamela immediately disappeared among the foliage.

182

"She's upset," Anita said. "She cared about him, to everyone's surprise."

"Yes." Imelda coughed. "It seems everyone did."

"Yes. What's happened is really dreadful."

Phyllida heard a sharp breath, but when Imelda spoke again her voice was still calm and clear. "The garden looks good from here, doesn't it, framed by the plants?"

"It looks beautiful." They were standing in a comparative clearing, and the long view across the lawn was confined in a serrated oval of hothouse greenery. Phyllida stepped back, to make Imelda Carrington a part of the picture, a figure in the landscape. . . .

And stepped back further, suddenly lightheaded, for the support of a seat.

Chapter Fourteen

Phyllida seemed to rest against the seat for a very long time, but when the world had steadied, Imelda was still gazing out at the garden, seemingly unaware of the loss of her companion. As she moved back to her, Phyllida told herself not to be a fool, but that didn't stop her seizing Imelda's hands.

"You have beautiful hands, honey." She had noticed them in the moment of meeting. As she raised them unprotesting in her own, the long, loose sleeves of the yellow blouse fell away, revealing a small gold watch on the left wrist and a thin snake of gold on the right. "Forgive me, but I notice hands," Anita apologised, as she let Imelda's go.

"So do I." Imelda looked bewildered as she spoke, as if remembering something from a distant past. "I notice hands. You have nice hands, too." After a quick glance downwards, her eyes had returned to space and she could have been reading from an autocue.

"Thank you." Phyllida was having to discipline her hands to stop them punching the air. Not that she had proof of what she persisted in being crazy enough to believe. Not yet. "Will you excuse me, Mrs Carrington, if I go upstairs?"

"Of course. As Bea said, please use my room."

Oh, but I will! Phyllida looked back from the doorway, and knew the frustration she would suffer if she failed to find her proof. And that if she succeeded some people could suffer the destruction of their lives.

184

Thelma and Deborah were picking their coats off the wide bed. If Pamela Bennett didn't decide to come upstairs as well, she would have her one chance.

"We think it's time we made a move," Thelma said to her. "It's been lovely but we've all had enough."

"I think you're right, honey. Don't wait for me, I'll be a few minutes. I'll see you both at the Gallery tomorrow."

"It's been great!" Deborah enthused, and Thelma looked abruptly solemn and gave Deborah's arm a shake for using the wrong word and tone.

Phyllida heard them on the stairs and didn't bother going into the bathroom. She crossed to the door to push it to, then sat down on the dressing stool, welcoming the reflection of the door in the wide sweep of mirror which would ensure sufficient warning for her to close an open drawer.

She blessed Steve for his insistence on teaching her to search with maximum thoroughness and minimum disturbance. Although her heart was racing and she was light-headed again, her fingers moved delicately and surely, discovering there were no jewel boxes in the drawer she had started with, opening the next one.

And finding it, under the first lid she lifted, solitary and snug in its shaped velvet nest. A Victorian gold bracelet set with opals and pearls.

Phyllida took it in her hand and knew she was holding it for the second time. Pamela pushed the door open when the drawer was safely closed and she was leaning on the dressing-table, trying to control the trembling that had now reached her hands.

"You all right?"

"I'm fine." Phyllida got to her feet. "Time to go, wouldn't you say? Oh, honey, I'm so sorry for you all." She put her hand on Pamela's arm, and it was not shrugged off.

"Thanks," Pamela said gruffly. "It's a ghastly dream."

Which would turn into a nightmare when Phyllida had done what she must.

"What shall we do for the rest of the day, my friend?" Philip asked her in the car.

She had been afraid of the rest of the day and still was, in an altered way. "I'm sorry, Philip, I really am. I'm tied up."

"I see."

"No, you don't." Suddenly she wanted to laugh, at the vast remove he was from seeing, but she also wanted to cry because of longing so painfully to stay with him, sleep with him, forget for one night at least both the past and the future. "It's not a date, Philip, it's a piece of business. I promise you."

"On a Sunday night?"

"On a Sunday night." She put her hand on his, on the steering wheel, and gave it what she hoped would feel like a friendly squeeze. "I'd rather spend the evening with you, but I can't. So if you'll take me back to the hotel."

"If you'll have dinner with me during the week."

"Of course." If Anita Sunbury was still around, if Imelda Carrington hadn't put paid to her.

As well?

"You all right?" He had felt her shudder.

"Just a goose on my grave. Thanks for squiring me today. Imelda Carrington's very beautiful, isn't she?"

"Yes." But he seemed puzzled. "Like a picture rather than a person, though. If that doesn't sound crazy."

"It doesn't." It sounded just right, the spot-on description of a woman who had numbed her emotions by a self-engendered anaesthetic because of the intensity of the pain. . . . "Is that how she always is?"

"I've hardly met her, but I don't remember thinking that before. I suppose it must be just having got over a migraine. Or not having got over it, and Being Brave."

"I suppose so."

"Which night?" he asked, as he drew up outside the Golden Lion.

"Wednesday?" He would be less difficult to deal with in the meantime if she made it soon, but the farther ahead it was the greater the possibility of Anita being unable to keep the appointment.

"All right. And perhaps next weekend. . . . Something companionable during the day? A drive in the country? A walk? A cream tea? I'd enjoy that too, you know."

Oh, so would I! But life would be a lot harder if she came to believe Philip Morgan capable of liking a woman as well as lusting after her. Her new knowledge could destroy some people, but it could deliver Phyllida Moon.

Peter wouldn't believe her.

"You're obsessed with that profile!"

"Perhaps I have been, but I really have found it. I saw it again against the window of the Carrington conservatory, and it belongs to Imelda Carrington. And the bracelet I saw and examined in David Lester's bedroom lives in her dressing-table drawer."

"Two female profiles. Two Victorian bracelets. There are plenty of both about, Phyllida, for heaven's sake."

"Yes, but these two are the same. I *know*. Believe me, Peter!"

He dropped his eyes before the glare of hers, and she turned her frustrated gaze on to the long, consoling view of the sea. When she had shed Anita she had walked the short way to the office because it was so near rather than because she expected to find Peter there on a Sunday afternoon.

But he had been snoozing on the rest room sofa

187

and, equally startled and defensive, they had met by Jenny's desk. Phyllida had asked him out of concern rather than curiosity why he couldn't keep away, and he had offered his usual non-macho response. "Oh, girlfriend difficulties. Reports to catch up with. And I like it here."

"So you're all right?"

He had grinned. "I promise."

But now, for the first time, they were at odds.

"Look," she said. "The last thing I want to do is tell Chief Superintendent Kendrick that Mary Bowden held out on him. But I have to. It's so important."

"Tell Kendrick?"

"Yes! And let him decide whether or not to tackle Mrs Carrington. If I don't do it we could be condoning the most awful miscarriage of justice."

"And if you do we could be ruining the lives of innocent people."

"Imelda Carrington isn't innocent. I mean, I don't know whether she is or not, but she told Anita she scarcely knew David Lester and yet I'm one hundred per cent convinced she was at his house last week. In the early morning. I'm not saying she spent the night with him, even though I smelled perfume on his bedclothes, and of course I'm not saying she killed him. I'm just saying that for some reason or other she was there."

"You didn't recognise the perfume too?"

"Of course not. But I recognised the woman in the taxi, and the bracelet. Peter, you know me well enough by now to have some confidence in my judgement!"

"But it isn't judgement, is it, Phyllida? It's just instinct. About which no one can be one hundred per cent convinced, you must know that." He got up and began pacing the room.

"It was instinct at first, but when I found the bracelet

it became a judgement. It was the same bracelet, Peter, and the same profile."

He wheeled round on her, met and held her determined gaze. "All right," he said at last, flinging back into his chair. "I'm not happy about it but I see I can't stop you so you'd better do it with my sanction."

"Thank you. And in your presence?"

"Oh, yes. I want to see Kendrick's reaction. To Mrs Sunbury rather than Mrs Cookson, I think?"

"So do I. Peter, I'm grateful."

"Don't be, it's only that I recognise a brick wall when I see one. And remember, I don't like it."

"I'll remember." Phyllida smiled at him, pleased to have discovered in her employer a willingness in certain circumstances to make himself disagreeable, an ability she had been half afraid he might not possess.

"You're at least prepared to wait until the morning?"

"Oh, yes."

In the morning, in Kendrick's office, Peter sat silent while Phyllida talked. But it was to him that the Chief Superintendent responded, as if Mrs Sunbury wasn't there. "She told you at the time, Dr Piper?"

"Yes."

"So why the hell didn't you tell *me*?"

"Because I decided it was a piece of the man's private life which was without significance."

Phyllida shifted in her seat and murmured protestingly. It had been her insistence that had kept the profile a secret, she hadn't even asked Peter if he had an opinion on what, if anything, they should do about it. But he subdued her with a hand on her arm and a severe glance.

"Murder victims don't have private lives," Kendrick explained wearily. "And the police, rather than the public, are the people to decide whether an incident is, or is not, significant. I'm grateful to you both for your help, but if you only tell me part of what you discover it can do more harm than good."

"It didn't seem like a discovery," Phyllida said. "And when Mary Bowden saw the taxi, David Lester was alive and her ethical problem was whether or not to report it to his sister."

"But then he was killed, and a taxi leaving his house at 9.15 a.m. with a woman inside it could have had a bearing on his death. . . . All right," Kendrick conceded. "You've come to me now because you've decided it could be significant after all, and I appreciate that. Mrs Sunbury – Miss Bowden. . . ." He had avoided addressing the elegant American for as long as possible because of not being sure how to cope with the unsettling realisation that if what she was telling him turned out to be true he would have to accept that she and Mrs Cookson were the same person. "You believe, following your visit yesterday to the Carrington house, that the woman you saw in the taxi was Mrs Carrington, and that the bracelet you found in the drawer of her dressing-table is the bracelet you found in David Lester's bedroom shortly before his death."

"I do. I recognised Mrs Carrington's profile when I saw her from a certain angle at her house yesterday, and the bracelet's very unusual – opals and pearls making small flowers like daisies. But I'm afraid my certainty that I'd seen them both before is all the proof we can offer you."

"We know that if you follow it up it's going to cause grief," Peter said, "and we're sorry to pass that on to you. Especially" – he glanced warily at Phyllida – "if it turns out there's nothing in it."

"That's my job, Dr Piper." Kendrick spoke the cliché with distaste, but it seemed to be the only possible response. He got to his feet. "Thank you both for coming in, I don't suppose it was easy."

190

"No," Peter said, as he and Phyllida rose too.

"Especially for you, Dr Piper," Kendrick went on. "Not having seen either the woman in the taxi or the bracelets."

"And having nothing to go on beyond female intuition," Anita drawled sarcastically. "And, there's only *one* bracelet, Chief Superintendent."

The three of them were smiling when the visitors left, and the smile remained on Kendrick's face as he lowered his long body back into his chair, despite his distaste for the immediate task ahead of him. It could be that a chink of light was showing for Paul Fisher, the tough young fraudster whose insistence that he was incapable of murder Kendrick now knew he believed. If one of Dr Piper's sidekicks was being hounded by her instincts, then so was he.

And they could both be right.

Kendrick rang for DS Wetherhead and told him the story.

"Charles Carrington will be at the Gallery, so straight to his house, I think," he finished, while his sergeant was still scratching his head. "Quietly at home, the minimum of disturbance, but making the connection out to be stronger than it is. I think we'll know right away if there is one."

"Yes, sir."

"Cheer up, sergeant." *Follow my example.* But they had to keep sight of the possibility that a liaison between David Lester and the wife of the Director of the Snaith Gallery could be no more than coincidental with Lester's murder.

And that Piper's women could have got it wrong.

"It's so *tidy* as it is, sir," Sergeant Wetherhead commented wistfully as he drove them slowly into the sunshine. "We don't *need* this." He slowed down further to swing into the Carrington drive. "And if she was walking into the sun on a day like today, as she admits she was, she'd've been too dazzled to make a reliable identification."

"Of course, Fred. That's why we have to overplay it."

DS Wetherhead whistled as they rounded the curve of the drive. "Nice, sir? And just look at that glass jungle!"

"Very nice, Fred," Kendrick responded absently. Although the air was crisply windless he shivered as he left the car, feeling suddenly draughty and as vulnerable at the top of his career ladder as he had felt on the bottom rung. And realizing there would never come a moment when he could say he had seen it all, except as an irony.

The modestly porticoed front door was opened by a small dark woman with a radiant smile. "Good morning! Can I help you?"

"Mrs Carrington?"

"Gracious me, no!" The woman was shocked by the sergeant's solecism. "But Madam is in. Who should I say?"

Both policemen had their IDs in their hands. "I'm Detective Chief Superintendent Kendrick of Seaminster CID, and this is Detective Sergeant Wetherhead. If Mrs Carrington could spare us a few moments. . . ."

"Please come in while I ask her." The smile continued undimmed and unwary. "Perhaps you'd like to sit there." She indicated a small sofa. "I shan't be long."

"The whole of my ground floor would fit into this hall," Sergeant Wetherhead observed conversationally, as his body relaxed into the pale gold brocade. Wetherhead was a good policeman, one of the best sergeants Kendrick had ever had, but there was an ultimate lack of sensitivity in him which Kendrick suspected could prevent his further promotion.

"Would it? Better leave it to me, Fred, initially," he suggested, as lightly as possible. "It's going to be tricky, and in one way or another it'll be painful as well. Ah!"

The policemen got to their feet as the tall figure appeared from the back of the house and walked slowly towards them.

"You want to talk to me?"

"If we may, Mrs Carrington." Kendrick took in the life-lessness of Mrs Carrington's pale, large-eyed beauty.

"In here, then." Mrs Carrington began to move towards one of the handsome white doors, putting out a hand towards its enamelled knob and making Kendrick think of a sleep walker. "You get off now, Bea," she said, turning in the doorway to the woman who was showing signs of accompanying them through it. "You've got a lot planned for today and I know you want an early start. I'll see you tonight."

Tactful, Kendrick commented to himself, as the dark woman said a reluctant farewell. He had been reacting to Mrs Carrington and, like Miss Bowden, realising that something was wrong.

"Please sit down." Mrs Carrington settled into a small armchair, and Kendrick and Wetherhead fitted themselves snugly into another two-seater sofa. Everything in the comparatively small room appeared grace-ful, feminine in an unsexual way. "And tell me why you're here."

"We're here in connection with the murder of David Lester." He couldn't have imagined her face paling any further, her eyes growing even larger. Her long thin fingers were gripping the narrow arms of her chair. "You'll appreciate that any information which could throw light on a murder, however unreliable or irrelevant it turns out to be, has to be followed up. Now, we have to tell you that you were observed leaving the house where

David Lester lived, The Cedars, in a taxi at about 9.15 on the morning before the night during which he was killed. My further information, which conflicts with that, is that you knew Mr Lester merely as a member of your husband's staff, and I shall be grateful if you can tell us the purpose of your visit to him. Hold on!"

Kendrick, who moved swiftly for so large a man, was across the room and catching Mrs Carrington by the shoulders before she could fall out of her chair.

Sergeant Wetherhead, too, was on his feet. "The other woman may not have left—"

"No!" Kendrick was glad to see that the heavy door was closed. "This could be a very private matter. Open that corner cupboard, will you, Fred."

Mrs Carrington's eyelids were fluttering and she was moaning when the DS said "*Eureka!*" and asked Kendrick to choose between brandy and Malvern water. "There are glasses, too!"

"Water, at this stage."

By the time the sergeant was across the room with it, Mrs Carrington had struggled upright and her eyes were open. Kendrick held the glass to her lips and she took it from him before drinking, spilling a little as she let him take it back.

"Thank you." She sank against the cushion, but her eyes remained wide. "I'm all right."

"D'you need any medication?" Kendrick asked. "Heart. . . ."

"I don't take medication. It was shock, Superintendent." Mrs Carrington gave a heavy sigh, and Kendrick saw her eyes come to life and be properly aware of him. "Please sit down, I really am all right. Just – sick with surprise. You see, I thought . . . I didn't think there was anyone who knew about David and me. Anyone in the world." Her eyes pleaded with him. Following their terrible emptiness, Kendrick had to welcome their misery.

"I'm afraid I can't tell you the source of our information, Mrs Carrington." It was one thing he would have liked to tell her, to spare her her search for an enemy. "But I hope you will tell us the reason for your visit to Mr Lester. Informally, at this stage. If it transpires that we need to – take it further – we'll do that at the station and what is said will be recorded. My sergeant will take a few notes now if you've no objection, but they won't constitute a statement from you at this juncture. All right?" She nodded. "So. The reason for your visit?"

"David and I loved one another and I'd spent the night with him." Her response was unhesitating. "I was able to because my husband was in London."

"Your husband doesn't know about your affair?"

"No, no!" She was desperately pale again, and Kendrick mouthed the word *brandy* at his sergeant. "David and I were going to tell him, because it was more than an affair and we wanted to spent our lives openly together. But I love my husband too and I wanted to choose the best time. . . . Not that there could be a best time, because he loves me . . . Oh, God, I thought when David died . . . I thought, at least, now, I don't have to crucify Charles."

"Drink this." Kendrick put the glass to her lips, and welcomed the hooding of her desperate eyes as she took it from him. But when she had sipped and coughed she raised them again to him, still pleading. "I'm sorry," he said, when he was back on the sofa. "I'm afraid your husband will have to be told."

"But it has nothing to do with David's murder!" She put the glass down on the table beside her and leaned towards him, holding out her hands. "And you've found his killer!"

"We've found the man who forged one picture by Frederick Sandys, and possibly two others. He denies the murder, and so far we've found no evidence to connect him with it."

"So you're looking for evidence to connect *me*! Well, you'll find my fingerprints, Superintendent. Most plentifully in the bedroom where I'm told David died. But that's all."

"Thank you. I'll be glad if you'll come to the station – later on – and let us take your prints for elimination purposes. Now, Mrs Carrington, did Mr Lester tell you he'd received two anonymous letters accusing him of responsibility for the forgery of the Sandys pictures?"

"He did. He was innocent, of course, but he was very worried by them."

"So why didn't he take them to the police?"

Imelda Carrington leaned back in her chair. "Chief Superintendent, you must see why. David was afraid he was being set up to take the rap for a fraud that would make headlines all over the world. It would mean media prying into his private life, the discovery of him and me before we were ready to tell Charles. If he'd told the police about the letters, the prying would have come from *you*, so he sat tight and hoped the letters might be a bluff. He didn't find that too hard, because of being so sure the Sandys were genuine, but he was desperately worried." A dry sob shivered the length of her body. "At least he was spared the verdict on *Winter*."

"Neither of you thought of pre-empting the danger by telling your husband about your affair? I'm sorry," Kendrick answered her reproachful look. "Your – love for each other?"

She leaned forward again, holding out her hands in the same pathetic gesture of entreaty. "Of course we did! But it was so difficult simply to meet, and so fraught when we did, we just hadn't come to any decision by the time. . . ."

"I understand," Kendrick helped out swiftly. "Mrs Carrington, you said just now that *of course* Mr Lester

196

was innocent of the fraud. Does that mean you have proof?"

"I don't need proof, I know – I knew – David!" Her anger had just managed to hold back the threatened tears as she changed tense, but one of them escaped and rolled down her cheek. "He had total integrity, he could no more have cheated on his vocation than he could have flown!"

Kendrick realised how tired he was getting of unsupported eulogies on the probity of David Lester. "Unfortunately your opinion isn't evidence, Mrs Carrington, but my sergeant is making a note of it." DS Wetherhead's lazy ballpoint accelerated. "Now, would you like to tell us how you and Mr Lester became – more than acquaintances?"

"About a year ago I went to a weekend seminar he organized at our local adult education college while my husband was abroad on business. It was Charles who booked me in because of my interest in pictures and my frequent lament that I don't know more about them." The brief twist of her lips gave Kendrick no clue to the quality of her normal smile. "A little gift to compensate for his absence. I'd met David at a few Gallery dos and thought, if I thought at all, he was a nice man. But that first evening . . . We talked in the bar after the opening session, sat together at dinner . . . He came to my room with a book we'd discussed . . . It was a *coup de foudre*, Chief Superintendent" – DS Wetherhead raised his pen, his eyes rolling – "but when the dust settled we saw that it made sense for us both."

"Which your marriage didn't?"

"Not after I met David," she said, again without hesitation, and Kendrick saw that he and his sergeant were in the path of the opening floodgates of a long reticence. "I loved Charles – I still love him – but it wasn't – it wasn't a necessity, it was something that

197

enhanced my life but didn't remake it. If David was beside me, the whole globe was. I'd have lived in a coalhole if he lived there too. No one can feel like that twice in a lifetime. I think – I know – that's the way Charles feels for me. So you see, Chief Superintendent, that now. . . ." Mrs Carrington closed her eyes, and tear tracks gleamed down both her white cheeks. "I don't mind what happens now," she murmured. "But I'd thought that at least my husband and I could carry on, and I was thankful for Charles's sake."

Until criminal justice disallowed even that one last satisfaction. "Mr Lester felt the same way you felt about your – association?" There had been more than one occasion in Kendrick's professional life when the motive for murder had been the fury of a woman scorned.

"Yes." The response was so matter-of-fact Kendrick decided it would have been difficult to achieve if it had been untrue.

"So you didn't kill him, Mrs Carrington. Did you kill him?"

"*What*?" She was on her feet. "Is this your idea of a joke? Are you sick?"

"I think you must answer the question, Mrs Carrington," DS Wetherhead intervened. "It's one we have to ask. As you'll appreciate when you can bring your commonsense to bear."

Imelda Carrington fell back into her chair, glaring at him. "I did not kill David Lester!" she flung at them.

"Thank you." Kendrick wondered if he was witnessing a reaction or a performance. He didn't have the same unnerving instinct for innocence he had more and more strongly when he was questioning Paul Fisher, but there was nothing telling him that Mrs Carrington was lying. "I'm sorry to distress you at such a difficult time for you, but as Sergeant Wetherhead said, that was a question which had to be asked. Now, can you tell me if Mr

Lester had any idea who the anonymous letters might have come from?"

"He had no idea at all. He went over it with me again and again, and there was no one he knew who seemed remotely likely. But all anyone needed to know about him to have sent the letters was his knowledge of the Pre-Raphaelites and his involvement with the recovered Sandys, so he decided it had to be a stranger. And it was a stranger who killed him, Chief Superintendent."

"We'll have to find out." Kendrick got to his feet. "Thank you for your frankness, Mrs Carrington. It's been very helpful and I appreciate it."

Imelda Carrington had also risen and was stumbling across to him, clutching his arm. "Mr Kendrick . . . please. . . ."

"What is it?" He steadied her with a hand round each shoulder.

"Please . . . You're going to tell my husband, you've said so, and of course I realise now . . . But please . . . May I have a little time to tell him myself first? It might just – save us. But otherwise . . . Please, Mr Kendrick. If I ring him now and ask him to come home. Then – keep him here – whether he wants to stay with me or not" – Mrs Carrington briefly closed her frantic eyes – "by telling him you're coming to speak to him . . . I shan't need long, I'll expect you back this afternoon. Early this afternoon! Please, Mr Kendrick!"

"Very well." He couldn't see it as a case where he had to be afraid of collusion. "We'll come back at two o'clock. Then take you to the station for fingerprinting."

"So you won't call at the Gallery?"

"No."

"Oh, thank you! Thank you!"

Kendrick ventured to remove his hands. "I hope it won't be too painful for either of you, and I'm sorry we can't keep your secret."

"And murder is murder. I know. I'm as anxious to find out who killed David as you are, Chief Superintendent, and I hope you find him first because if I find him there could very well be a second death."

The beautiful eyes flashed, and the soft voice slid round steel. If it was a performance it was a brilliant one.

"I'll find him, Mrs Carrington. And I'll see you at two o'clock."

Her anger carried her on firm feet to the front door, but as she closed it on them Kendrick found himself feeling uneasy about her.

So, clearly, did Sergeant Wetherhead. "She's not up to the ordeal," he pronounced, as he drove between the gateposts.

"She has to be, Fred. And we have every right to go straight round to the Snaith Gallery."

"I know, I know, and I'm glad you decided we wouldn't. But you've got your murderer, sir. Waiting for you in an interview room."

"Perhaps." It was as near as he had got to voicing his instinctive doubts about Fisher, and he felt the driver's seat jerk under his sergeant's reaction.

"Perhaps?"

"I'm still thinking about Barney Barnes's office. How it put me in mind of David Lester's house."

DS Wetherhead cleared his throat, preparatory to the delicate exercise of disagreeing with his superior. "I'd have said one going over was much like another, sir."

"Maybe," Kendrick answered mildly, so busy with his thoughts he had scarcely heard what his sergeant had said.

"The media's getting restless about Barnes by the way, sir, the feeling is it's time we had someone helping us with our inquiries into that murder, too. And we don't have a clue, we can't even put them off with a Press conference."

"Not at the moment, no. You'll have read about the Wallace case, Fred?"

"I can't just recall it, sir."

"Wallace was the man from the Pru. An insurance agent whose wife was murdered while he was out looking for a non-existent address he'd been asked by telephone to call at for some business. That was in the early thirties, and fifty years later new evidence was found to suggest that the real murderer had set Wallace up by sending him on a wild goose chase the other side of Liverpool."

"And you think someone set Fisher up? Told him to stay at Lester's flat?"

"It happened in 1931, Sergeant. It could happen again."

"But, sir." DS Wetherhead cleared his throat again. "It seems to me a lot more likely Paul Fisher just made the story up to give himself an alibi."

"That's how it seemed to the police who arrested Wallace."

"So who could have set Fisher up, sir?"

"I haven't the faintest idea, Fred. It just strikes me that his alibi is as absurd as Wallace's for another man in his apparently right mind."

"What happened to Wallace?"

"He was convicted, but escaped the gallows because it was deemed on appeal that the evidence against him was insufficient and unreliable. Which it now appears it was."

"No gallows on the horizon for Fisher, which makes it all a lot more relaxing. It's just struck me, sir," the sergeant said almost excitedly, as he accelerated away from a brief hold-up, "how much more fraught it must have been for everyone, not just the murder suspect, when the outcome of all their deliberations and decisions could be judicial death."

It wasn't the first time DS Wetherhead had come out

with an apocalyptic phrase, which could be part of the reason Kendrick always found himself interested in his sergeant's reactions. "You have to be right, Fred, at least we're spared that responsibility."

But not the sense of weary frustration which, as they drove through the glittering morning, Kendrick found himself fighting off as if it was a suffocating blanket. He succeeded in the moment of realising, with extreme distaste, that there was one thing he could, and would, do immediately.

Chapter Fifteen

"A telephone call for you, Mrs Sunbury!"

Phyllida quickened her strolling pace towards Reception.

"Will you take it here or shall I transfer it—"

"I'll take it here. Thanks, Deborah."

"Safe to talk?" Peter asked.

Deborah was handing out leaflets.

"Briefly."

"Right. Tell them someone important to you is ill and asking for you. Then get to the hotel and ring me on your mobile."

"Right. Oh, God, is it serious?" She had raised her voice.

"Not life-threatening," Peter said.

"Thank heaven for that." Phyllida paused. "Yes, I'm sure I can, expect me inside an hour. Goodbye. Deborah!" The urgency in her voice cut into Deborah's animated chat and she whirled round. "Look, that was bad news about a friend of mine. She's had a heart attack and she's asking for me. I'd like to go to her."

"Of course, Mrs Sunbury! Goodness, I am sorry!"

"So am I, honey, and I'm sorry to have to leave you like this."

"Don't *worry*! I'll cope."

"I know you will. Now, I'll just have a word with Mr Carrington."

But Thelma told her Mr Carrington had left the gallery

about half an hour earlier. "He had a telephone call from his wife," she said, her plump face puckered with anxiety. "Apparently she wasn't well and asked him to go home. They had a little chat and he shot off looking really upset. I do hope it's nothing serious. I must say I didn't think she was quite herself yesterday."

"She'd had a migraine, hadn't she? Perhaps it's got worse again and she wanted him with her. I'm afraid I must go off too, honey, I've just heard that a close friend has had a coronary."

"Oh, *dear*! Is she in Seaminster General? If she is I can—"

"She's in south London. I'll be as speedy as I can, Thelma, but I can't see myself getting back to work today."

"Of course not! We'll manage. Luckily we've got no special exhibition on at the moment, and the public interest in David's death seems to be dying down." Thelma's eyes flashed scorn, then smiled protectively as they met Anita's. "Take care, dear. Will you drive?"

"Yes. And I'll take care. Thanks, Thelma. Expect me tomorrow if I don't call you."

Phyllida walked the short way to the Golden Lion as briskly as possible without attracting attention, and punched out the office number on her mobile phone as she entered the narrow corridor leading to her room.

"What is it, Peter?"

"It's Kendrick. He's letting Mrs Carrington tell her husband about her affair with Lester before the police call on him. In fact the police are calling on them both at home at 2 o'clock this afternoon. He wondered if you could go round in the meantime on say a door-to-door market research survey and get some idea of how they're doing. His request came at the end of a very long pair of tongs and he made it plain this wasn't a blueprint for the future, but he seems to realise we've been fairly useful on

this case and might just be able to do something more. So
– an unremarkable woman of whatever age you decide is
most appropriate. And as quickly as you can. Leave your
car in the road. And if there's anything likely to be said
that Kendrick would wish to hear, switch your recorder
on and leave your bag open if you possibly can. I'll send
Jenny over to Reception with a clipboard and paper, plus
any likely looking bumf we can turn up."

"Thanks." She had already discarded the Anita wig
and was using her free hand to start work on her face.

"Look. . . ." Peter's fluency faltered. "If I don't hear
from you by 1 o'clock and can't contact you, I'll come
and join you."

"That suggestion frightens me a little. Did the Chief
Superintendent make it?"

"No. So don't worry, for goodness' sake. It's only that
I look after my staff."

"So thanks. But I hope I'll be ringing you before one
o'clock. It's only a quarter past eleven."

Twenty minutes later, the sort of woman no one
remembers announced herself at the Golden Lion Reception counter as Dr Piper, and was handed a large
envelope. In the car Phyllida discovered the package was
headed by a pristine questionnaire on consumer spending,
fortunately undated, justifying Jenny's invariable refusal
to throw away anything that "might come in handy".

It had been coldly sunny when she left the Gallery,
but as she drove out of the carpark some spots of rain
spattered the windscreen and the few streaks of blue
began to disappear behind lowering grey cloud. Phyllida
got out of the car a few yards short of the Carrington
gates into a chilly wind, glad of the drab, head-hugging
wig with its tight French pleat.

On foot she found the drive long, but it allowed
her time to control an uncomfortable acceleration of
her heart beat. Charles Carrington's car stood close to

the front door, but there was no reply when she rang the bell.

She rang it fruitlessly two more times, then set off round the house to the conservatory, wanting to skulk her way among the bushes and having to force herself to walk normally in the centre of the path.

At first, when she reached the door, she saw nothing but the lush and varied greenery. Then, as she peered under her raised hand and cut off some of the reflection from the garden, she noticed the tall, elegant figure of Charles Carrington standing in motionless profile as his wife had stood the day before, apparently studying an exotic bush.

Against all her instincts Phyllida lowered her hand and knocked on the glass.

Charles Carrington showed no reaction, but when she knocked again his body jerked and he turned to face the door before walking slowly towards it and turning the handle.

"Hello," he said as he opened it. It had not been locked. He looked beyond Phyllida to the strengthening rain. "You'd better come in before you get too wet."

"Thank you. I'm doing a door-to-door survey on patterns of consumer spending and I wondered – A-a-g-h!"

Phyllida had followed the Director of the Snaith Gallery round the first leafy corner, and stretched out on the tiles in front of them, lying on its back with its head to one side, was the body of a woman. Phyllida's first realisation was that the woman was dead. The face was suffused purple, the tongue between the lips, and she needed a few more ghastly seconds to recognise Imelda Carrington.

Charles Carrington had stopped beside his wife's body, and looked back at Phyllida as she staggered to a seat.

"As you see, I've just strangled my wife," he said, with his usual grave courtesy. "I'm sorry to have given you such a shock. No, I don't think so," he went on more quickly, as Phyllida struggled back to her feet and turned towards the door. "I don't think you should leave until you've calmed down. And until I've talked to you, I need to talk. Don't worry," he said as he came back to her after locking the door, the key in his hand. "I'm not going to strangle you too, there'd be no point in it. I don't care what happens to me now Imelda's gone, and the police will be here at two." Phyllida found herself still able to be shocked by the sudden crumpling of his face. He sank down on the seat opposite the one where she was crouched and from where she could see one of Imelda Carrington's elegant and motionless feet, the toes still inside the pale shoe. Wriggling along towards the shelter of a bush, she was just able to lose it from the corner of her eye. "I hadn't meant to kill her," Charles Carrington explained. "I'd thought, now Lester's gone, we'll carry on as we were, she'll go on loving me the way she always did – not the way I loved her, the desperate way – but the love I'd settled for. She told me she'd never stopped loving me that way, but then she told me about the way she loved Lester, the real way, the way I love her, and I couldn't bear it, I couldn't listen, I had to stop her. Oh, God, Imelda. . . ."

When he had gone to lock the door, Phyllida's shaking hand had just managed to open her bag as Peter had suggested and switch on the tiny receiver.

"Do go on," she said softly, amazed at the calmness of her voice. "It always helps to talk to a stranger, I've found that myself."

"Yes!" He looked eagerly across at her, and her one solace was to see that he was aware of her as no more than a pair of ears. Perhaps as no more than his own thoughts, wanting to get themselves into order. "You see," he said, settling into his seat. "Although I knew she was having an affair with Lester I didn't know she loved him the way I loved her, I didn't know that. When she told me,

207

I knew right away we could never go on together the way I'd thought we could when I first knew what was happening and decided to get rid of him."

"You decided to kill David Lester?"

"Oh, yes," he said, as if it was the most natural thing in the world.

To express her horror would be to squander her terrible opportunity. And perhaps make him aware of her as more than his inner voice. "How did you find out about his affair with your wife?"

He showed his surprise. "Because of loving her, of course. When you love, you notice. She thought she was hiding it, but I knew she'd turned away from me. So I got someone to follow her and he took photographs." *Barney Barnes*. The earlier shocks had failed to anaesthetise her against this one. "I went through the tortures of the damned." Not, Phyllida realised on a wave of nausea, because of remorse at what he had done to Barney. "But I was angry. It helped me, my anger, it helped me to do what was necessary. To punish Lester for his wicked presumption!"

So it had been a mixture of outraged pride and unmanageable love that had done for David Lester. Phyllida tried not to cower as Carrington's memory of his anger brought him to his feet, although she still clung desperately to her hope that he would remain unaware of her as another human being. "So you thought it was all down to him."

Carrington glared across the tiles as he sank back into his seat. "Of course it was! Imelda would never. . . . He made her love him, you see, it was like witchcraft, she couldn't help it. And I killed her. Oh, God, I killed my darling Imelda!" Phyllida watched in silence as the pride came back. "But I had to kill her, what else could I have done when she told me that?"

"Let her go." If she was right, and he was aware of

her only as the other half of an internal dialogue, she wasn't being all that brave.

"She had nowhere to go!" he cried wildly. "Had she?"

"She could have gone away."

"Without David Lester?" he demanded scornfully, and Phyllida decided she had seen the first and last flicker of his conscience.

"Tell me about the pictures," she invited. "Did David Lester have anything to do with the faking of the Sandys?"

"Of course not!" The pale eyes danced, and Charles Carrington pressed his hands together in excitement. "I chose Sandys for two reasons: because he was in David's field and so when I killed him everyone would assume the scam was the reason for his death and not look beyond it. And because, as well as painting *Autumn*, Sandys made the *Spring* sketch and announced his intention of working it up and painting *Summer* and *Winter*, which meant the experts would be predisposed to accept Fisher's work as genuine. I could have sent him the wrong materials right away, but I knew how good he was and I wanted to help the Gallery by presenting *Spring* and *Summer* as genuine – as they'd arrived anonymously, the Gallery's reputation wouldn't have suffered if my experts had rejected them. I thought I could take my time, you see, I thought I had as much as I wanted, that Imelda would tire of David. I didn't know she was planning to leave me." Carrington's mouth twisted, and he closed his eyes and arched his back as if resisting physical pain. "But my ultimate goal was David's death, and I began working towards it from the moment I had Barney's first report."

"How did you meet Paul Fisher?"

"A couple of years ago he punished a dealer who turned his work down by offering him a phoney Lord Leighton. He didn't admit to painting it until the dealer had bought it and shown off to the media. When I decided to kill David I bought one of Fisher's Rossetti copies, and it would have taken me in if I hadn't known Fisher had painted it. His telephone number was on the back of the picture, as well as his name and address, so there was no need to come face to face with him."

"So what did you do?"

"I rang him calling myself Lester and speaking from the chest." Carrington laughed reminiscently. His eyes were on Phyllida as if she was one of the exotic bushes surrounding them, not seeking or meeting hers. "It's an accomplishment I discovered as a child and used as a party piece. It hurts after a few moments but it's effective, makes one sound like a Dalek. I told him what I wanted and that I'd send him the contemporary materials and enough money to ease his conscience, and he agreed. That's what I did for *Spring* and *Summer*, and for *Winter* I sent him modern materials, so that when the picture went to the experts they'd discover it was a forgery."

"That was clever. And I suppose you sent David Lester the anonymous letters to connect him with it."

"And to create a tension in him which would show up as guilt. That was clever, too." *Too clever*, Phyllida silently amended. If he hadn't sent them Mrs Cookson wouldn't have gone to The Cedars and his scheme would have succeeded. "The way I expressed the letters and put them together, they pointed to someone less sophisticated than the Director of the Snaith Gallery being privy to what he was doing. But he disappointed me." A shadow crossed the calm, self-satisfied good looks. "I'd hoped he'd tell the other members of staff, but he kept them to himself and probably destroyed them, they weren't anywhere in his house or his office and I'd wanted the police to know about them. Not that they were more than the grace notes, you might say, to my grand scheme."

"You'd have wanted to see the pictures before they went to the Gallery. How did Fisher get them to you?"

"Ah!" Again the excited clasping of the hands. "I own a complex of holiday flats on the promenade, and last summer David rented one for his sister's family. I rented it anonymously after his tenancy expired, and I sent Fisher a key and told him to put the pictures inside it. Then, on a routine visit, I locked myself into the flat, vetted them at my leisure and parcelled them up. Then posted them at the general post office at busy times. As the flat had been rented by David, I wasn't afraid of Fisher talking to the police, I wanted him to. And I wanted him to give them the absurd alibi I'd created for him for the night David died."

"You'd read about the Wallace case."

"Of course. Richard Gordon Parry – the man who killed Julia Wallace after sending her husband off on a wild goose chase – Parry was my inspiration. He got away with it for fifty years. Until after his death. When I killed Imelda I thought I'd killed my chance of measuring up to him, but I'm beginning to see I still could. . . ." For the first time Charles Carrington looked towards his wife's body. Then back at Phyllida, and for a hideous moment saw her.

"So you told Fisher to go to the flat that night." If she allowed herself to think about what could happen she would be incapable of lengthening the odds against it.

"Yes! It was like taking sweets from a baby. He was so eager to meet the mysterious Lester I could have sent him anywhere. I stayed behind in the Gallery when everyone else had gone, as I so often did, and I printed Fisher's name and address on David's computer, put it inside a folder he'd handled, and put the folder into the bottom drawer of his filing cabinet. I'd seen on an earlier night that the key to the drawer was lying in the space made by the drawer handle – David never locked anything –

so it was more child's play to lock the drawer and take the key away. I turned his house over to make sure there was nothing in it about – him and Imelda – for the police to find. The one thing I slipped up on was not knowing his sister was away. I should have checked on that. After killing David I'd intended making enough noise to bring her out of her room and then use the knife on her because of her having seen me. It was a shock to find her room empty, and I had a bad time until I could be sure David hadn't confided in her." Phyllida struggled to turn her retching into a cough. "Killing Mrs Everett would have fitted for Fisher as well, and he would have turned the house over to make sure there was nothing in it about his part in the scam. So you see—*What's that?*"

Phyllida's mobile had beeped from inside her handbag and she brought it out, clamping the bag shut on her other device. "My HQ," she said, forcing herself to smile reassuringly. "If I don't ring in every—"

"No, I don't think so." He was across the space before she had seen him get up, taking the mobile from her hand. "You see," he said as he laid it on his table and sat down again, covering it with his hand, "I'm beginning to think life might still be worth living after all, so I may need you to help me prepare a grave for Imelda so that I can tell the police she went away. If I do that, I shall have to put you into it as well. You see that, don't you?"

"Yes." *Oh, Peter!* Phyllida forced her trembling hand to unlatch her handbag, then glanced at her watch. When she had managed to focus it she saw it was a quarter to one.

"So where was I? Oh, yes." A shudder passed over him. "The thing that really hurt me was having to damage that exquisite furniture."

So it was the Director of the Snaith Gallery rather than Miss Bennett who preferred things to people. "That night. . . ." It came out as a moan, and Phyllida cleared her throat and tried again. "That night, didn't your wife know you'd gone out?"

He smiled serenely. "No. I only got back from town at eleven." A long way away, Phyllida saw a picture of Thelma Royle, telling the occupants of the staff rest room that her boss was about to go to London. "Imelda was waiting up for me and we had a nightcap together. I'd heard from Barney Barnes that day that she'd spent the previous night at The Cedars" – for an unnerving moment Charles Carrington's face was a mask of fury that was not reflected in his voice – "and I knew she'd be tired and that the strong sleeping pill I put into her whisky would keep her asleep until I got home. In fact, she didn't waken till I was leaving for the Gallery next morning. And of course I had no worries that she would suspect me, because she had no idea I knew what she was doing. She hadn't noticed the change in me, you see, the way I'd noticed the change in her."

"Yes, I see," she whispered, and saw also that he had noticed her looking again at her watch.

"Yes," he said, getting to his feet. "It's time I got on with things, the police will be here in just over an hour and I must be finished by then so that I can tell them Imelda's left home." He smiled ruefully across at her, still not seeking her eyes. "I'm afraid there's another reason I must bury you with her. You see, although talking to you has helped to clear my mind and I'm very grateful, there was one thing I shouldn't have told you."

He was looking for a response and she heard a voice whisper "Yes?"

"I shouldn't have told you all the Sandys are fakes."

The voice said, "The police will know that from Paul Fisher." Phyllida wanted to get up, to run to the door and bang on it and shout, but she was unable to move.

"Oh, yes, he's proud of them. But the police won't believe him, they'll think it's vanity. I mean, that's what

213

he would say, isn't it? You don't have an axe to grind, there's no reason for you to say they're fakes, unless you know they are, so they'll believe you, or at least lose their certainty that they're genuine. So you see, I have to kill you for the sake of the Gallery, whatever I decide I want for myself. I'm very sorry." He was coming round his table, had paused halfway across to her. "I think the wild bit, beyond the vegetable garden. You'll have to help me carry Imelda."

She couldn't get up on her own but he was helping her, taking her by the arms and hauling her to her feet. Putting his hands round her throat when she was upright, then murmuring, "Imelda first," and taking them away. Staring towards the door behind her and snarling his rage as the first pane broke, releasing Phyllida from her paralysis so that she spun round and went racing the short way to freedom, seeing Peter's fair head behind the hat of the policeman who was destroying the door, and screaming as she ran.

"I shouldn't have left my bag behind," she apologized, when she had been lying for what felt like days on the squidgy velvet sofa in the Agency rest room, flanked by her employer and two fellow members of staff. She had asked to be taken there rather than the little room at the Golden Lion, or home. Or hospital, which the police had suggested.

"Carrington was in no state to investigate it," Peter said. "I've just had Kendrick on the phone and he tells me that by the time the police reached him he was having a stroke."

"So you'd have been okay," Steve reassured her, and Jenny told him to shut up.

Peter's vigil had been intermittent, and as Jenny and Steve hadn't stirred from her side, it occurred to Phyllida that he had been operating a one-man service.

214

She struggled upright. "I'm all right now."

"Lie down!" Steve ordered masterfully. Jenny put a gently restraining hand against her cheek, and Peter perched on the arm of the sofa.

"The tape's very good," he said. "And very valuable. Kendrick didn't put it quite like that, of course, but it's on the cards Carrington won't be able to talk again and he was obviously pretty grateful. I suspect there was some remorse there too for having sent you into the lion's den, so we've piled up quite a bit of credit." Peter paused. "I'm sorry I let you go, Phyllida. But with Fisher in custody. . . ."

"I know, I didn't think either, although I felt a bit tense and reluctant when I was walking up the drive." Her shudder was involuntary but it upset Jenny, who told them sternly they'd do better not to talk about it.

"It's all right," Phyllida said. "And I'm glad everyone will know about Carrington." She yawned, realizing she felt sleepy. But not wanting, yet, to sleep on her own. "Please go back to work," she told them. "But keep looking in on me."

Jenny kissed her before, with anxious backward glances, they trooped out. She reappeared quite soon, looking embarrassed and followed by a man Phyllida hadn't seen before, who turned out to be Peter's GP. When he had had a look at her and taken her blood pressure he gave her an injection and told her to go on resting, and when she next opened her eyes it was dark and she shouted in panic.

Peter was there instantly, flooding the room with light.

"I'm sorry," she said, pleased to feel the smile on her face. "What on earth time is it?"

"It's nine o'clock," he said, as if it was his fault. "You must be ravenous. How d'you feel?"

"Much better," Phyllida said truthfully, as she lowered

her legs to the floor. "Just stiff and thick-headed. And sorry to have kept you here so late."

"Don't be smooth, you know that most evenings I'm here more often than not anyway. Take your time in the king of bathrooms, and then we'll go and get something to eat." As part of his suite of rooms Peter had taken possession of a bathroom with Victorian fitments, including a vast claw-footed bath, which he loved to distraction and vigorously protected from Jenny's longing to bring the room up to date.

He watched Phyllida anxiously as she got to her feet. "All right?"

"Fine." Any problems would come later, when she was on her own.

"D'you want to talk about it?" he asked her, when they were seated at a scrubbed table in his favourite small French restaurant.

"I don't want to make a point of not doing. I think I'd like to know whether Carrington's a psychopath, or his obsession with his wife just got out of hand, but perhaps they won't be able to find out, now. Oh, Peter, I'm glad to think his body's trapped him, that he's his own last victim. I'm glad!"

"Everyone is. Except perhaps Steve, who'd have preferred to despatch him compos mentis in a vat of boiling oil."

"He told me the thing that really upset him was having to damage The Cedars furniture. So perhaps his wife was the only human being who was real to him."

"Which would make his love for her a pretty dangerous thing."

"Yes." Phyllida put her knife and fork together. "That was delicious, it's just that I don't feel as hungry as usual. Peter, in the theatre you can live through the most heart-rending drama and then it's absolutely over and no one goes on suffering. In this job there are so many sad

216

loose ends. Mrs Everett lonely and unhappy in that big house – and you and I only able to hope she never finds out what Carrington had planned for her. And it has to be the end of the Snaith Gallery. And maybe of Thelma Royle."

"And Paul Fisher will come out of prison as famous as Thomas Keating."

"But Imelda . . . If I hadn't seen her in the taxi she wouldn't have told her husband that she really loved David and she'd still be alive."

"Living with the monster who killed her lover."

"She wouldn't have known . . . Oh, Peter, I don't know!"

"You have to let them go," he urged her. "We do our best to help people, but once a case is closed we can't go on feeling responsible for them or we'd be crushed. Believe me, Phyllida."

"I'll try to." She looked round the room and then pointed to her glass, her heart pounding. "I'll have some more wine, please."

"What a good idea. And I'm driving you home. I asked Steve to collect your car, by the way, you'll find it there when you get—"

"Thanks. Look, Peter, there's Philip Morgan. It'll be interesting to see if he gives me a second glance."

Philip had helped his young and pretty companion into her seat and was now smiling across the table at her and taking her hand before raising his eyes above her head and looking swiftly round the room, pausing en route on the face of another attractive woman. But not at Phyllida Moon.

The sort of man who would always be alert for something better than the thing he had. Well, that had been her judgment at the start and she should be glad to have it confirmed: she had lost him anyway, and it was better to be left without regrets.

"He wasn't even puzzled," she said with a laugh, as she watched Philip raise the girl's hand to his lips. And, to her relief, she really was finding it funny.

"I told you you were a good actress. I thought he was supposed to be madly in love with Mrs Sunbury, by the way."

"So did I. He was very convincing." Phyllida laughed again, without effort.

"Oh, well." Peter shrugged and raised his glass. "To your TV career, dear, and to your career with the Agency. That's still on, isn't it?" he asked with sudden anxiety, halting his glass at his lips.

"It's still on." Despite what she knew awaited her in the solitude of that night, would await her on future nights when she had walked away from more desperate and broken people, perhaps lucky again to have escaped with her life. "It's still on, Peter!"